LEVEL ONE QUESTIONS

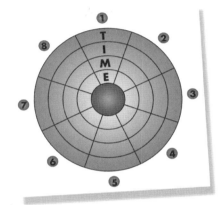

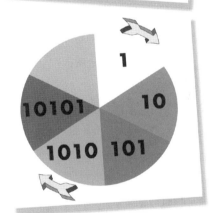

W	I	N	S		
W	I	N	e		
W	I	N	i	n	g
W	I	N			
W	I	N			

1. RUNES _____
2. TROUT _____
3. ANDREW _____
4. MOANS _____
5. CHEATER _____

1. PAINT BOX

Fill in the boxes using the letters R, G, Y and B. Each row across, each column down and each diagonal from corner to corner must contain a R, G, Y and B square.

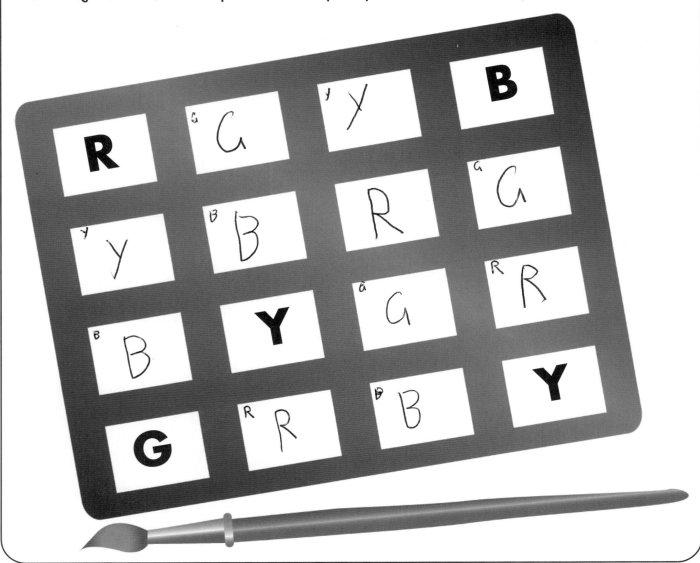

2. LINKS

Which word will go after the first word and before the second word?

QUICK(s a n d)CASTLE

3. CLOCKWORK

If the big and small hands changed positions, which clock would show the latest time in the same twelve hour period?

A

B

C

4. CREATURE CODE

Letters have been replaced by shapes. The first group spells out the word BEAR. Using the symbols from the first word, can you crack the code and work out what the other symbols are?

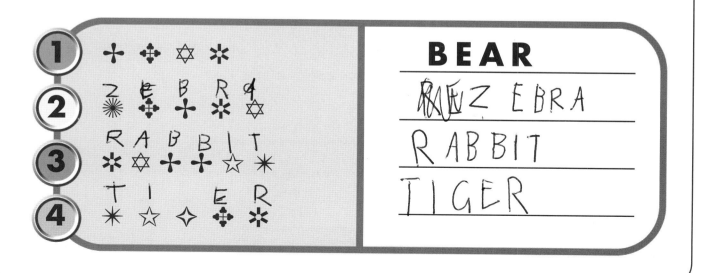

BEAR

~~RAEZ~~ Z EBRA

RABBIT

TIGER

5. BIRTHDAY

A girl is looking forward to her birthday. one of her best friends has a birthday the month before, and another good friend has a birthday the following month. All these three girls have the same name as the month in which they were born. What's the name of the girl who is looking forward to her birthday?

May

6. TOP TEN

complete the word by filling the spaces with a whole number between ONE and TEN.

1 6 4 2 10

H O N e S T

8 9 5 3 1

7. ADDER

Using other words with the same meaning, can you create a new word from two separate ones?

        ROD, RAIL
+   **LINE**
_____

=   **HANDCART**

+   _ _ _
+   _ _ _
_____

=   _ _ _ _ _ _

8. UNWANTED

You have to fill the frame using the words in the list, starting from TIP which is in place at the top of the frame. All words contain THREE letters, and there is only one way possible to fill the frame. When the grid is complete there is ONE word that has not been used. What is the unwanted word?

AIR
COW
CRY
DIP
EYE
FEW
FOG
GUN
IMP
MOO
OAK

PAW
ROW
SAD
SKI
TAR
TIP
WAS
WIN
YES
YOU

9. PIC-TRICK

Which single three-letter word completes all of the words below?

```
        _ _ _ R O V E
    S H R _ _ _
    L _ _ _ I N G
    _ _ _ _ L Y I N G
```

10. SECRET SEVEN

Rearrange the letters in the word below to make another word of seven letters.

C A S T E R S

Actress

CLUE

Think MOVIE STAR

11. CASUALTY!

These four people have all had accidents and visited the hospital. Can you name each one and work out the order in which they called at the hospital?

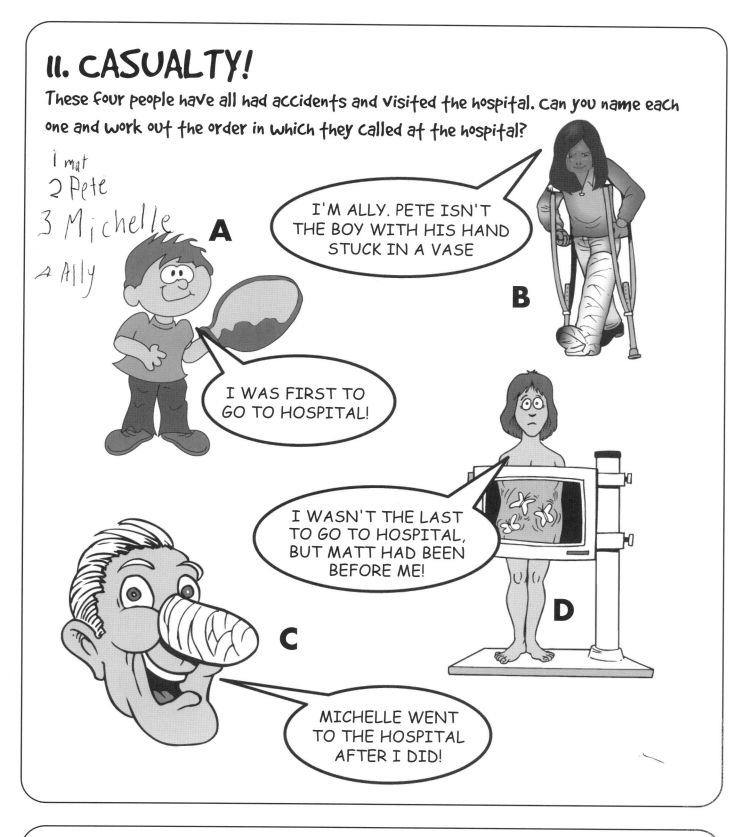

12. MORE OR LESS

Which is the higher number, the number of days in April or the number of months in two and a half years?

13. EYE CHART

Write your answers reading across the rows. Each answer is made by rearranging letters of the line above with one extra letter added.

- ○ First letter of the alphabet
- ○ You are, I _____
- ○ Adult male
- ○ Complain
- ○ From Ancient Italy
- ○ Dark shade of red

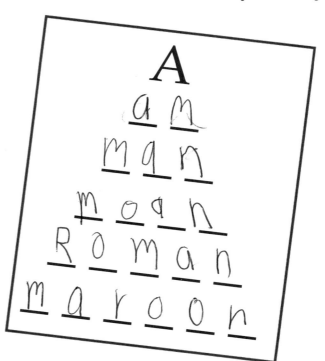

A
a m
m a n
m o a n
R o m a n
m a r o o n

14. LINK LETTERS

Put a letter in each of the sets of brackets which can be added to the end of the first word and the start of the second word. The first one uses the letter P, to make CRAMP and PINK. The five letters in order will spell out another word.

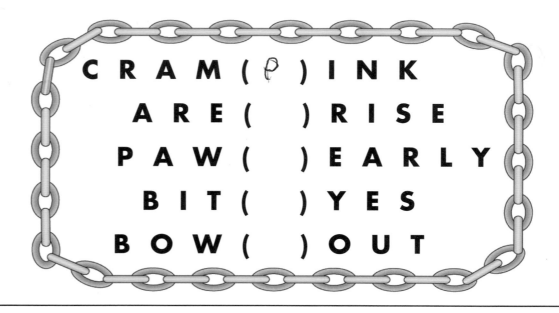

C R A M (P) I N K
A R E ( ) R I S E
P A W ( ) E A R L Y
B I T ( ) Y E S
B O W ( ) O U T

15. SPLITZER

Split this row of ten letters into two five-letter words which are the names of musical instruments. The words read from left to right and the letters are in the correct order.

F O L R U G T A E N

16. STAR GAZING

Which other telescope contains the same nine stars as seen in the telescope?
Look out, the stars are NOT in the same positions in the pattern!

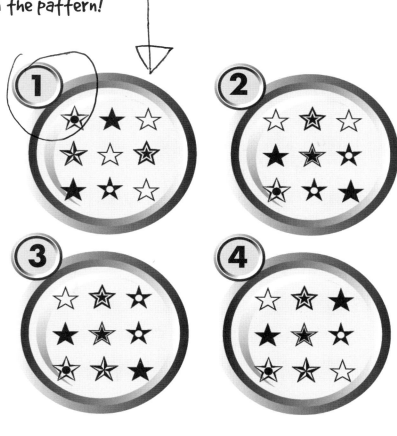

17. AFTER WORDS

Which word can go after all these words to make new words?

LIGHT House

GREEN House

DOG ~~Green~~ Caver

~~Dog~~ Dog Killer

18. JUST THE JOB

Start at the letter N, top left. Move from letter to letter, going in any direction, except diagonally, and spell out the names of five different jobs. You will use every letter once.

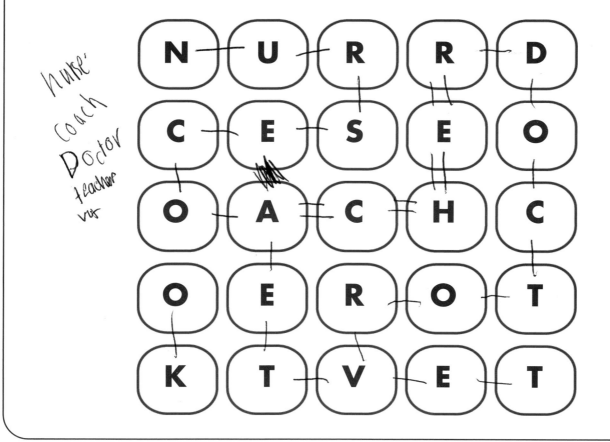

nurse
coach
Doctor
teacher
vet

19. NUMBER RING

Starting from the arrow and moving around the circle, can you work out the correct number to go in the blank section, to continue the number pattern?

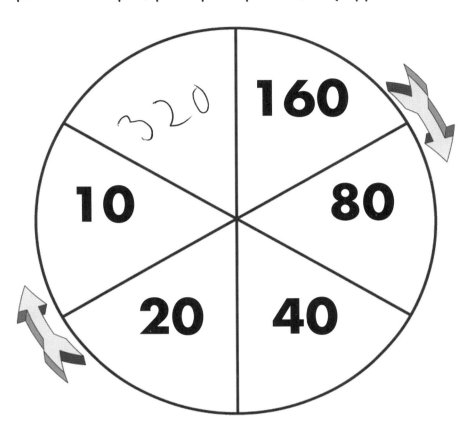

20. SECRET SEVEN

Rearrange the letters below to make a seven-lettered word.

E A D H R E D

R e d H e a d

CLUE

Think HAIR COLOUR

21. LINKS

Which word will go after the first word and before the second word?

TABLE (<u>t e h n i s</u> **) RACKET**

22. TRI-TANGLE

How many complete triangles can you count in the pattern?

23. TOP TEN

Complete the word by filling the spaces with a whole number between one and ten.

6 4 2 10

C O N <u>t</u> <u>e</u> <u>n</u> **T**

9 5 3 1

24. FIRST CHANGE

Each clue has two answers. The two answer words are spelt the same, except that the first letter of the second answer has moved forward one place in the alphabet. So for example, if the first answer was BAT the second answer would be CAT.

THE THING HIT IN TENNIS * **SHOUT OUT OR YELL**

ANSWERS: _____ / _____

CUT A LAWN * **THIS INSTANT!**

ANSWERS: _____ / _____

BEING WELL KNOWN * **SPORTING CONTEST**

ANSWERS: _____ / _____

A STYLE OF DANCING * **BELONGING TO ME!**

ANSWERS: _____ / _____

THE SHAPE OF A CIRCLE * **NOISE**

ANSWERS: _____ / _____

25. TWO TIMER

All the listed time-linked words are hidden in a letter grid. Each appears in a straight line that can go in any direction. One word appears twice in the grid. Which word is it?

THE LIST

AFTERNOON
DAY
HOUR
MORNING
MINUTE
NIGHT
NOON
SECOND
TIME
WEEK

M	T	N	O	O	N	D	B	U
N	O	A	L	A	W	H	A	D
O	V	R	A	D	O	E	O	Y
O	M	I	N	U	T	E	E	P
N	S	L	R	I	L	N	M	K
R	B	E	M	X	N	I	E	P
E	T	E	C	U	L	G	G	R
T	H	I	H	O	E	H	O	E
F	O	W	M	L	N	T	R	A
A	Z	E	B	E	P	D	X	L

26. ADDER

Using other words with the same meaning, can you create a new word from two separate ones?

LIMB

+ BELONGING TO US

_ _ _

_ _ _

———————————

= PROTECTIVE CLOTHING

_ _ _ _ _ _ _

27. MAZE CRAZE

To read the message, move through the maze from START to FINISH. You have to take a path that calls at every letter and you cannot go to the same letter more than once. There are four words in this piece of sound advice!

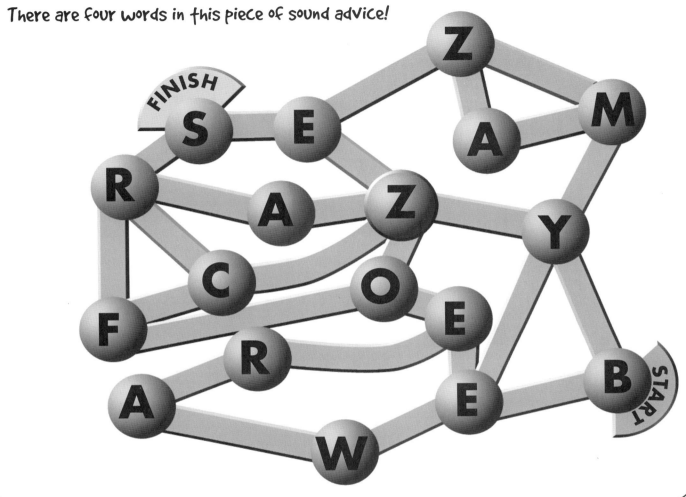

28. BACK WORDS

Solve the clues: the second answer is the first answer written backwards.

STICKY HAIR FIXER   *   LIMB

_ _ _   *   _ _ _ _

29. CUBED

A word square reads the same whether you look at it across or down. Use the listed words to make two different word squares. Use every word once with CUBE appearing in each word square.

ABLE	BLUE	CUBE	CUBE
EYES	REEK	SCAR	UGLY

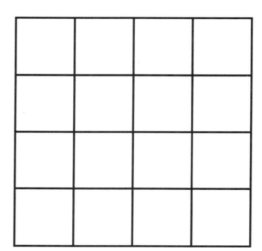
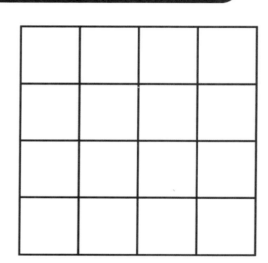

30. REALLY WILD!

The names of these wild animals have had the letters rearranged.
Can you sort them out?

1. A B R E
2. O N L I
3. S N E A K
4. G R I T E
5. A B R E Z

6. T E L P N A H E

31. WHAT AM I?

My first is in slam
But isn't in lamp.

My second is in made
But isn't in damp.

My third is in pace
But isn't in pale.

My fourth is in real
But isn't in sale.

My fifth is in dies
But isn't in born.

My last is in toil
But isn't in worn.

What am I?

32. LINE-NINE

The nine lines are arranged in a pattern containing three triangles. By moving the position of just three lines, can you form a pattern that contains five triangles?

33. MIND THE GAP

Which single three-letter word completes all of the following words?

H _ _ _ E R

T R _ _ _ S

R E P _ _ _ E D

C H _ _ _ I N G

34. HIT LIST

Noah Lott has set up his own information website. He's been up and running for five days. The first day was pretty quiet, but there's been more activity as the week has gone on. In fact, each day he has had 6 more hits than on the previous day. By the end of day five a total of 100 people have visited the site. How many had called at the end of the first day?

35. AFTER WORDS

Which word can go after all these words to make new words?

B A L L _____

B A T H _____

B E D _____

36. BRUSHSTROKES

Pick up these seven paintbrushes, labelled A–G, one at a time. You can only move the brush that is on top of the pile at each go.

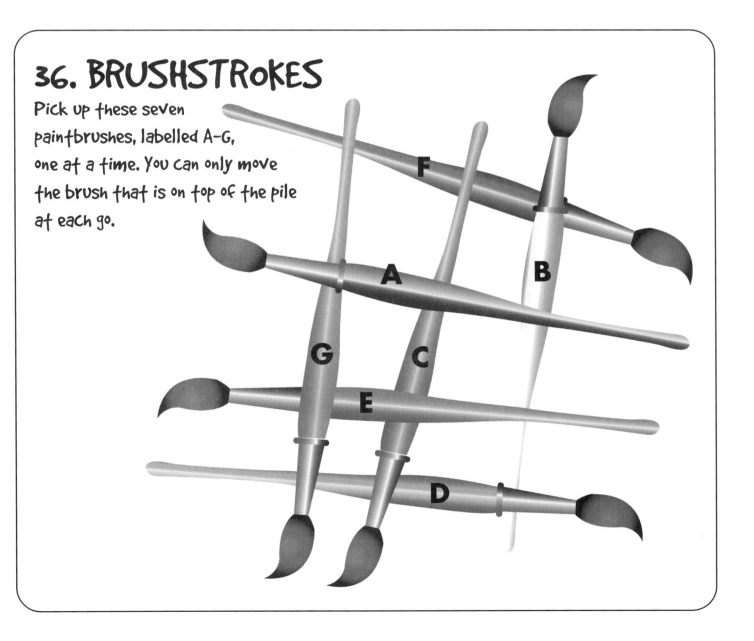

37. SECRET SEVEN

Rearrange the letters in the word below to make another of seven letters..

A D M I R E R

_ _ _ _ _ _ _ _

CLUE

Think
HUSBAND AND WIFE

38. HALF TIME

Each answer is a word containing four letters. The last two letters of one word are the same as the first two letters of the next word.

1			
2			
3			
4			
5			
6			
7			

1   Middle of an apple

2   A short break

3   Mix in with a spoon

4   Part of the eye

5   Island

6   Go in front in a race

7   Eve's partner in the
    Garden of Eden

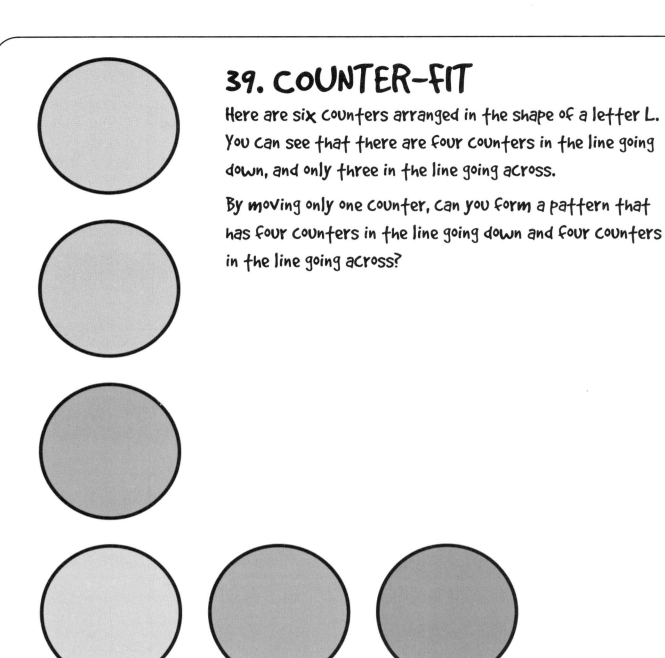

39. COUNTER-FIT

Here are six counters arranged in the shape of a letter L. You can see that there are four counters in the line going down, and only three in the line going across.

By moving only one counter, can you form a pattern that has four counters in the line going down and four counters in the line going across?

40. LINKS

Which word will go after the first word and before the second word?

BASE (_ _ _ _) GOWN

41. LOCKER ROOM

Forgetful Fran's forgotten the number on her locker. Can you work out which one it is?

- ◯ It is directly above a locker that has a black door.

- ◯ It is directly below a locker that has a black handle.

- ◯ Fran's locker has a white handle.

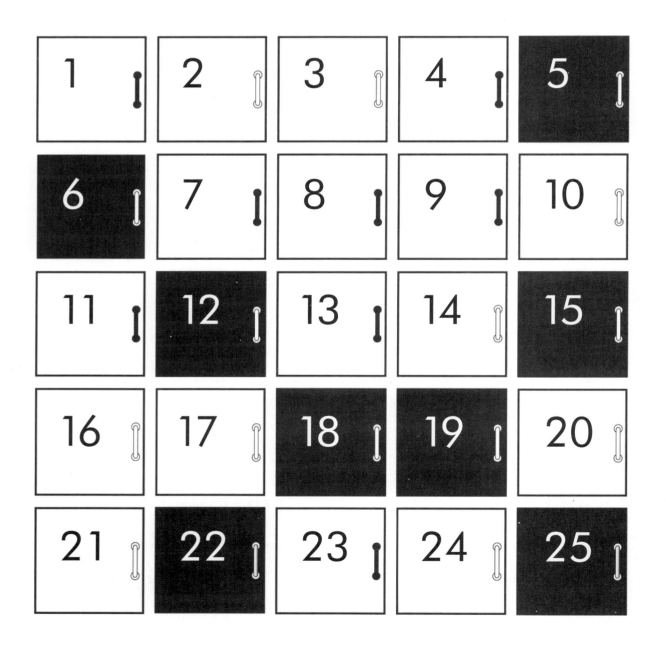

42. SPLIT UP

The words below have been split in half and the ends moved around. Can you repair the splits?

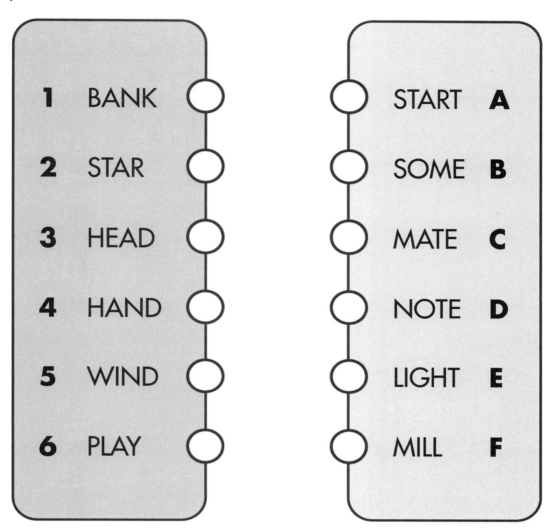

1	BANK	○	○	START	**A**
2	STAR	○	○	SOME	**B**
3	HEAD	○	○	MATE	**C**
4	HAND	○	○	NOTE	**D**
5	WIND	○	○	LIGHT	**E**
6	PLAY	○	○	MILL	**F**

43. BACK WORDS

Solve the clues: the second answer is the first answer written backwards.

WATER BARRIER * **CRAZY**

— — — * — — —

44. FRUIT MACHINE

With each spin this fruit machine always shows a banana, cherries and a bunch of grapes. There's only one more combination to those shown here. What is it?

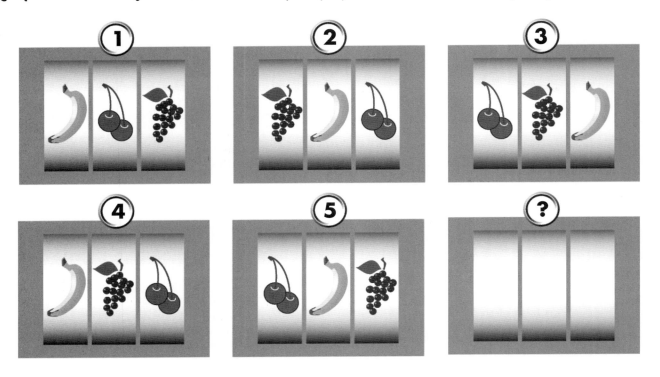

45. ADDER

Using other words with the same meaning, can you create a new word from two separate ones?

CRAWLING INSECT   _ _ _

+ EDGE OF A SKIRT   _ _ _

= HYMN   _ _ _ _ _ _

46. VOWEL PLAY

The vowels – A, E, I, O and U – have been taken from the names of these capital cities. Can you work out the names?

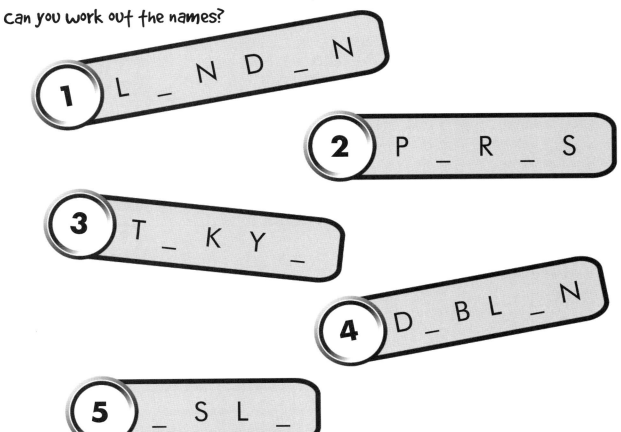

1. L _ N D _ N
2. P _ R _ S
3. T _ K Y _
4. D _ B L _ N
5. _ S L _

47. SIDEWAYS

Which is greater, the number of sides in 16 triangles, or the number of sides in 12 squares?

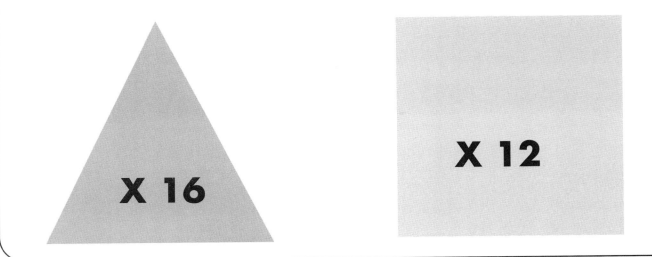

X 16

X 12

48. SECRET SEVEN

Rearrange the letters in the word below to make another word of seven letters.

A D V E R T S

_ _ _ _ _ _ _

CLUE

Think WITHOUT FOOD

49. JOBSWORTH

Rearrange the letters in the words below to spell out names of different jobs.

1 RUNES _____

2 TROUT _____

3 ANDREW _____

4 MOANS _____

5 CHEATER _____

50. ROWS AND ARROWS

Move one square at a time to get from start to finish. You must move in the direction the arrow is pointing. If the arrow points in two ways then you can go in either direction.

Start

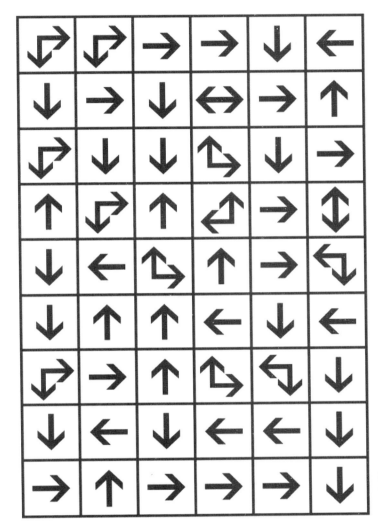

Finish

51. SPLITZER

Split this row of ten letters into two five-letter words which are the names of animals. The words read from left to right and the letters are in the correct order.

P T A N I G D E A R

52. WINNERS

Using the clues below, fill out the table with the correct answers.

1. **W**	**I**	**N**		
2. **W**	**I**	**N**		
3. **W**	**I**	**N**		
4. **W**	**I**	**N**		
5. **W**	**I**	**N**		

1. Air current
2. Used by a bird in flight
3. Area of glass in a wall
4. Blinks with one eye
5. Drink made from grapes

53. CHILL OUT

Turn HEAT into COLD by changing one letter at a time and making a new word with each move.

1	H	E	A	T
2	__	__	__	__
3	__	__	__	__
4	__	__	__	__
5	C	O	L	D

54. NUMBER TRAIL

Which line contains numbers that will add up to exactly 50?

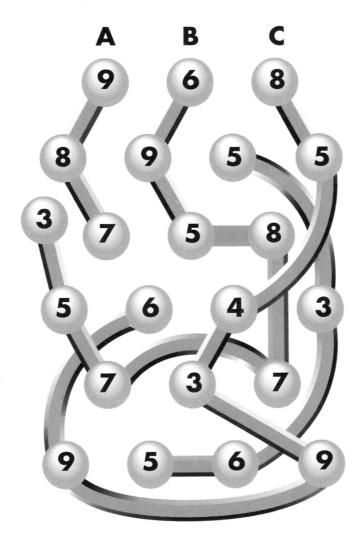

55. AFTER WORDS

Which word can go after all these words to make new words?

HALF _____

LIFE _____

SOME _____

56. TIME TURN

Solve each clue and write the answers into the spaces in the grid. All answers have four letters. Put the first letter in the outer circle, then move towards the centre. Only one letter changes between answers, and answer eight will be only one letter different from answer one.

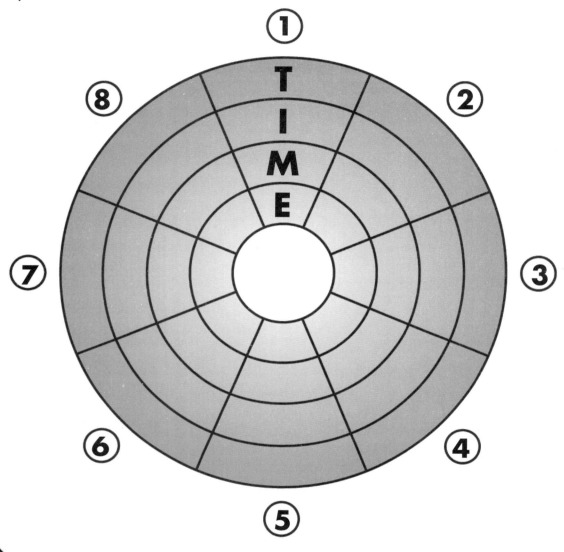

1. Measured in hours and minutes **2.** Not wild
3. Exactly alike **4.** A few but not everything
5. The bottom of a shoe **6.** Goods at bargain prices
7. A story **8.** Square covering for a bathroom wall or a mosaic floor.

57. TOM'S TASTES

Tom has strange tastes in fruit flavours.

He likes to eat an orange but not a satsuma.

He would eat a peach but not a nectarine.

He would eat a lemon or a lime but not an apple or a pear.

Can you say why?

58. SECRET SEVEN

Rearrange the letters in the word below to make another of seven letters.

R E L A T E D

_ _ _ _ _ _ _

CLUE

Think CHANGED

59. HORSE CODE

In this code each letter of the alphabet has been replaced by a number. H O R S E is written as 8 15 18 19 5. Work out how the code works and then fill in the grid. When you've cracked the code, have a laugh at the joke!

23	8	1	20
W	H	A	T

4	15	5	19
D	O	E	S

1
A

8	15	18	19	5
H	O	R	S	E

3	1	12	12
C	A	L	L

1
A

2	1	4
B	A	D

4	18	5	1	13
D	R	E	A	M

? ?

1
A

14	9	7	8	20	13	1	18	5
N	I	G	H	T	M	A	R	E

60. PIC-TRICK

What phrase is shown here?

S P L O S T A C E

61. BACK WORDS

Solve the clues: the second answer is the first answer written backwards.

PLACE FOR RUBBISH * PEN POINT

___ ___ ___ ___   *   ___ ___ ___ ___

62. SHADY

Answer each question with a five-letter answer reading across. When you have all the answers in place the centre shaded column reading down will reveal part of a computer.

1. Ciphers

2. Flower to make chains

3. Another word for glue

4. Abbreviation for microphones

5. Computer link to phone line

6. Mistake

7. Transfer from a computer on to paper

8. Stored in the computer's memory

9. A reward

63. WORLD TOUR

Rearrange the letters in the words below to spell out the names of countries.

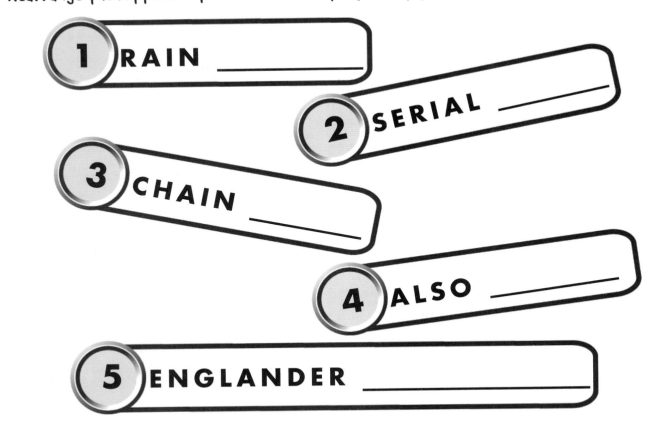

1 RAIN _____

2 SERIAL _____

3 CHAIN _____

4 ALSO _____

5 ENGLANDER _____

64. NEW IDEAS

Using the listed words, make three word squares which read the same across and down. The word IDEA appears in each square.

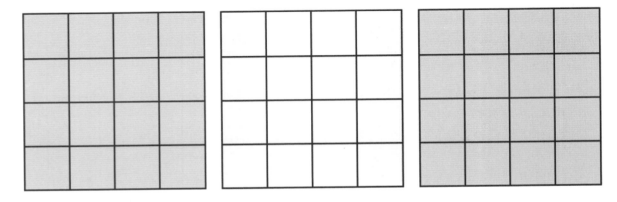

ARTS, DEAR, EAST, EATS, IDEA, IDEA,
IDEA, NEST, PEAR, PINE, RODE, TRIP

65. MIND THE GAP

Which single three-letter word completes all of the following words?

_ _ _ _ T A G O N

O _ _ _ _ I N G

S _ _ _ _ D

_ _ _ _ C I L

66. ADDER

Using other words with the same meaning, can you create a new word from two separate ones?

TREE _ _ _

+ METAL _ _ _

= ON LAND BY THE SEA _ _ _ _ _ _

67. INVISIBLE COLOUR

Most of the letters of the alphabet are shown here, but some are missing. Work out which letters are not shown here. These letters make up the name of a colour.

68. NUMBER-RING

Starting from the top arrow and moving around the circle, can you work out the correct number to go in the empty section, to continue the number pattern?

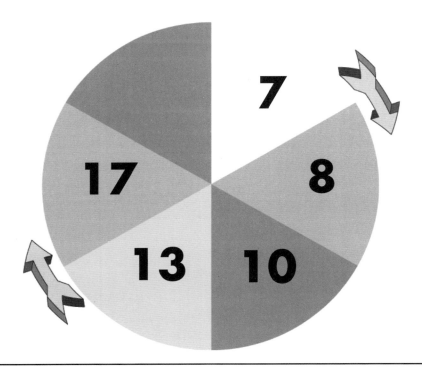

69. AFTER WORDS
Which word can go after all these words to make new words?

C H E Q U E _____

P H O N E _____

S C H O O L _____

70. INSTRUMENTAL
The name of a musical instrument is hidden in each of the sentences below. Find them by joining words or parts of words together. The first is done for you.

1. Have a wasH OR No one will get anything to eat!

2. It was a loud, rumbling noise.

3. I hate to cancel long established invitations but I must.

4. A goose or gander is in the garden.

5. The trip Ian organised was a tremendous success.

71. TOP TEN

complete the word by filling the spaces with a whole number between ONE and TEN.

6 2 5 8
10 1 4 9 3 1

A R _ _ _ R K

72. SPLITZER

Split this row of ten letters into two five-letter words which are the names of meals. The words read from left to right and the letters are in the correct order.

L S N U N C A H C K

73. BACK WORDS

Solve the clues: the second answer is the first answer written backwards.

MARRY * MOISTURE ON THE GRASS

_ _ _ * _ _ _

74. SAIL AWAY

Which of the sails shown on yachts 1, 2 and 3 carries on the pattern made by A, B and C?

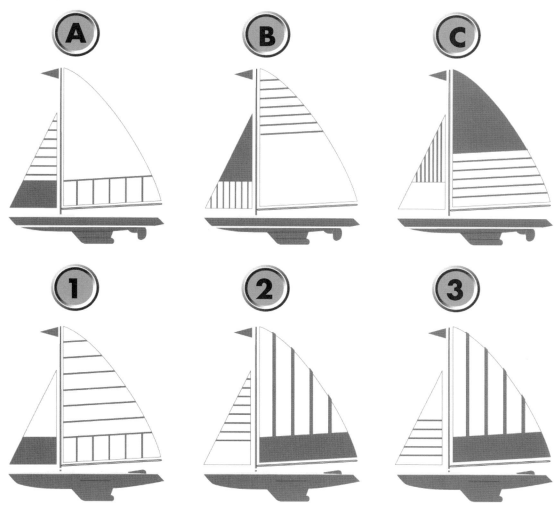

75. LINKS

Which word will go after the first word and before the second word?

P E A N U T (_ _ _ _ _ _) F L Y

76. CODED NUMBERS

Shapes and signs have been used to take the place of letters of the alphabet. Can you work out what the words are? They are all numbers and the first word is TEN.

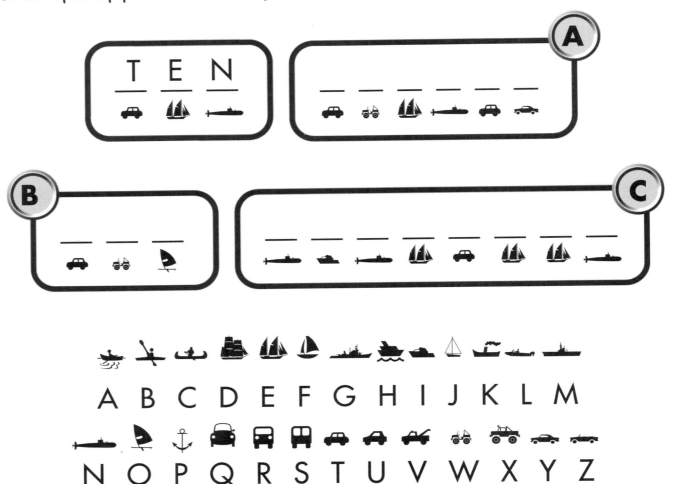

77. MORE OR LESS

Which is the greater amount – the number of years in a century, or the number of sides in twenty four squares?

78. WRITING ON THE WALL

The groups of letters are arranged in alphabetical order.
Move them around to spell out words connected with Egypt.

1 M M M U Y

_____

2 A D I M P R S Y

_____

3 B M O T

_____

4 A C E L M

_____

5 D E E R S T

_____

79. SECRET SEVEN

Rearrange the letters below to make a seven-lettered word.

L A R G E L Y

CLUE

Think
ART MUSEUM

80. CONNECTING ROOMS

Can you find your way through the maze?

START

FINISH

81. CALENDAR COUNT

What is greater - the number of days in January and December, or the number of months in five years?

OR

2012
2011
2010
2009
2008

82. GO FOURTH

What links these groups of words? Find out and complete the third group!

The first group of words is:

V	O	T	E	■	O	B	O	E	■	T	O	I	L	■	E	E	L	S

The second group of words is:

G	A	S	P	■	A	C	H	E	■	S	H	I	N	■	P	E	N	S

The third group of words is:

R	O	B	E	■	O	M	E	N	■	B	E	A	D	■				

83. AFTER WORDS

Which word can go after all these words to make new words?

FULL _____

HALF _____

HONEY _____

84. NUMBER RING

Start from the top arrow and move round the circle. You have to write a number in the blank section that will continue the number pattern.

85. FOOT FIND

The name of an item of footwear is hidden in each sentence below. Put your best foot forward and find them by joining words or parts of words together.

1 The gardeners hoe the flowerbeds.

2 Rob hurt his lip, perhaps, when he fell over.

3 On the beach the sand always gets in between my toes.

86. TOP TEN

Complete the word by filling the spaces with a whole number between ONE and TEN.

AT _ _ _ TION

87. ADDER

Using other words with the same meaning, can you create a new word from two separate ones?

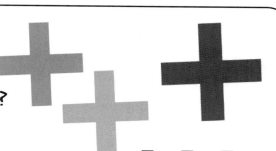

   JEER _ _ _

+ GOLF PEG _ _ _
_____

= BABY'S FOOTWEAR _ _ _ _ _ _

88. FRUIT FRIENDS

Five friends select their different favourite fruit.

Each friend names a different fruit.

Each friend has three letters in their own name that appear in the name of their favourite fruit.

Can you match friends to the fruits? There's only one possible solution!

Geena

Grapefruit

Lizzie

Lime

Melon

Paula

Orange

Neil

Peter

Tangerine

89. BACK WORDS

Solve the clues: the second answer is the first answer written backwards.

PINCH   *   METAL FASTENER

_____ _____ _____ _____ * _____ _____ _____ _____

90. SQUARE EYES

How many squares are there in this pattern?

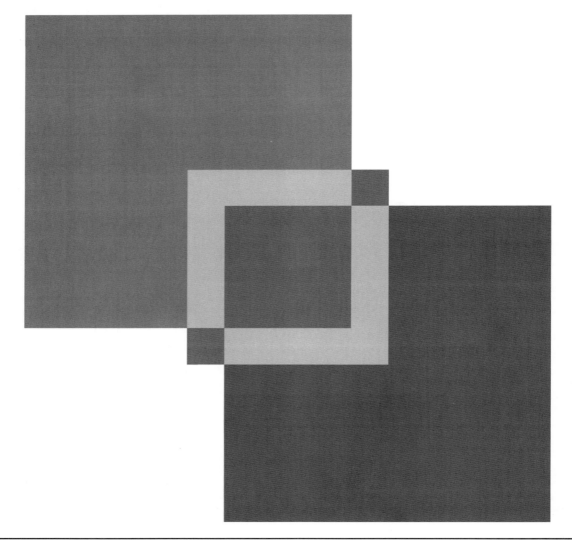

91. LINKS

Which word will go after the first word and before the second word?

FALSE(_ _ _ _ _) CLOCK

92. PICK A CARD

Four playing cards, one of each suit and all of a different value, are set out in a line.

There are no picture cards.

The diamond is the lowest value, with the card to its immediate left worth one more. These two cards, along with another card, total the value of the club, which is not on the outside of the line.

The red card on the left is equal to the value of the two lowest cards. The red cards add up to six less than the value of the black cards. What are the four cards and in what order are they arranged?

93. SECRET SEVEN

Rearrange the letters in the word below to make another word of seven letters.

A N G R I E R

_____
_ _ _ _ _ _

CLUE

Think
JEWELLERY

94. BREAKER

The words below have been broken in half and the ends moved round. Can you repair the breaks?

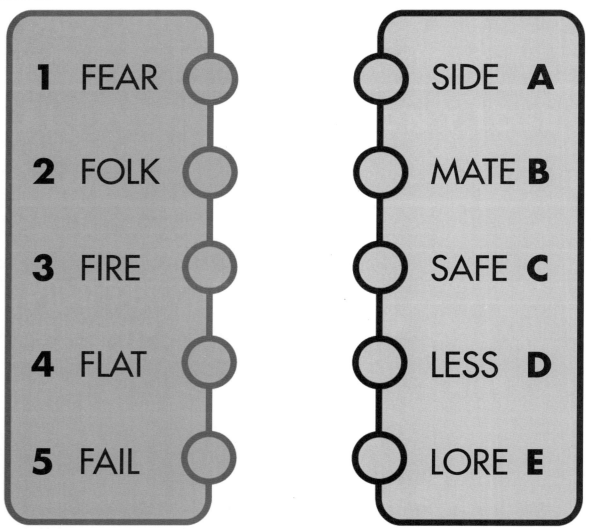

1 FEAR

2 FOLK

3 FIRE

4 FLAT

5 FAIL

SIDE **A**

MATE **B**

SAFE **C**

LESS **D**

LORE **E**

95. MIND THE GAP
Which single three-letter word completes all of the following words?

_ _ _ C H

T O _ _ _ O

C L I _ _ _ E

_ _ _ _ E D O R

96. COMET CODE
Symbols have been used to replace letters of the alphabet. The first group form the word COMET. Can you work out what the other space-linked words are?

1. ✦ ★ ★ ✦ ✳   C O M E T

2. ★ ★ ★ ★   _____

3. ★ ✦ ✳ ✦ ★ ✳   _____

97. SPLITZER

Split this row of ten letters into two five-letter words, which are the names of countries. The words read from left to right and the letters are in the correct order.

C E H G Y I N P A T

98. TON UP

Can you move from the top row to the bottom row so that the numbers on your route add up to exactly 100? Start from any number on the top row. Move down from row to row, always going to a number that is directly below, or to the left or right of the previous number.

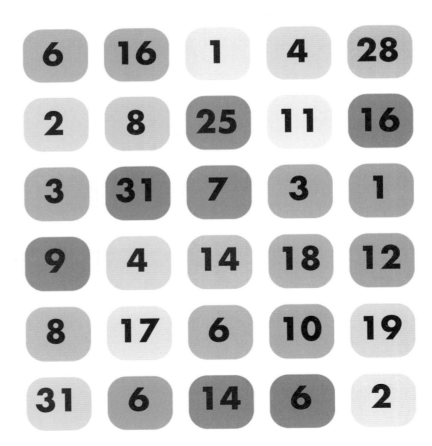

99. LADDER

Turn the top word into the bottom one, altering one letter with each step and forming a new word each time.

TENTH

PLACE

100. TIME TOTAL

Which is greater - the number of years in a century and a half, or the number of minutes in two and a half hours?

101. ADDER

Using other words with the same meaning, can you create a new word from two separate ones?

MOTOR VEHICLE   _ _ _
+ GO BAD   _ _ _
_____
= VEGETABLE   _ _ _ _ _ _

102. KID'S STUFF

The name of a young animal is hidden in each of the sentences below. Find them by joining words or parts of words together.

1 I pick identical shoes to my friend's.

2 I don't know when the ecu begins to be legal currency.

3 Jill ambled along the lane with her friends.

4 I'm going to chop up some wood for the fire.

103. STRANGE SUM

Letters have taken the place of digits in this addition sum. Replace the numbers so that the sum will work.

$$YZX$$
$$+YYX$$
$$\overline{ZYY}$$

$$\_\,\_\,\_$$
$$+\,\_\,\_\,\_$$
$$\overline{\_\,\_\,\_}$$

104. MIND THE GAP

Which single three-letter word completes all of the following words?

S _ _ _ C H

C U S _ _ _ D

S _ _ _ T L E

_ _ _ G E T

105. AFTER WORDS

Which word can go after all these words to make new words?

F O X _____

B L O O D _____

W O L F _____

106. TOP TEN

Complete the word by filling the spaces with a whole number between ONE and TEN.

D _ _ _ _

107. TIME TWISTER

Can you unscramble the groups of letters to spell out words connected with measuring time?

1 Y A D _____

2 R U O H _____

3 K E W E _____

4 D E C O N S _____

5 T I M U N E _____

108. TV SALES

There are only three TVs left in the sales rack from a 16-rack display. From the clues, can you work out the position of each one?

1 There are no TVs left in row 4.

2 There are no TVs left in column B.

3 There are two TVs left in row 3 and they are side by side.

4 There is one TV in column A but it isn't in the top corner.

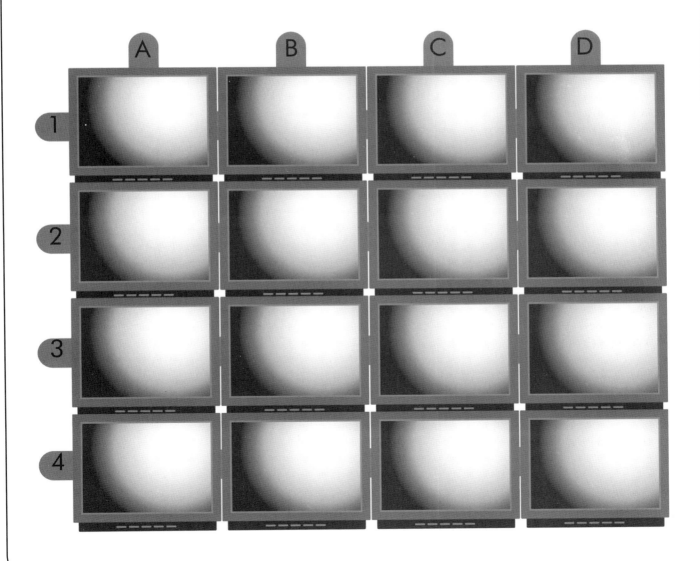

109. SECRET SEVEN

Rearrange the letters below to make another word of seven letters.

R A W N E S S

_____

_ _ _ _ _ _ _

CLUE

Think
REPLIES

110. PLAY THE SYMBOLS

Symbols have been used to take the place of letters of the alphabet. The first group of symbols stands for the word TRIANGLE. Can you work out the names of the other musical instruments using the same code?

1) ✳❋☆✡★✦✪✤   **TRIANGLE**

2) ✩☆✡★✦

3) ★❋✦✡☆

4) ✦❋☆✳☆❋

111. BACK WORDS

Solve the clues: the second answer is the first answer written backwards.

MESH   *   A NUMBER

___ ___ ___ ___   *   ___ ___ ___ ___

112. LINKS

Which word will go after the first word and before the second word?

S K I M M E D (_ _ _ _) S H A K E

113. DOCTOR, DOCTOR!

A well-known doctor in London had a brother living in New York who was also a well-known doctor. However, it is well-known that the well-known New York doctor did not have a brother in London who was a doctor.

How can this be?

114. SPLITZER

Split this row of ten letters into two five-letter words which are connected with home entertainment. The words read from left to right and the letters are in the correct order.

R A V I D E D O I O

115. DAYS MAZE

Which is greater – the number of days in June, July, August, or the number of days in September, October, November?

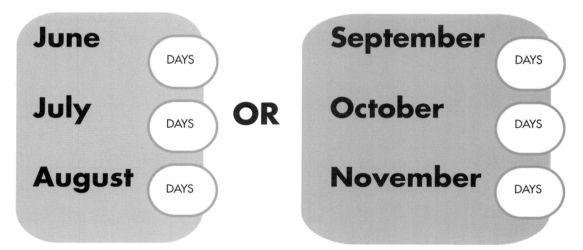

June — DAYS

July — DAYS

August — DAYS

OR

September — DAYS

October — DAYS

November — DAYS

116. ADDER

Using other words with the same meaning, can you create a new word from two separate ones?

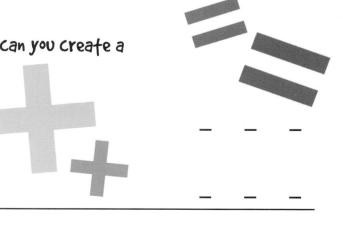

TIN
FRENCH WORD
+ FOR 'NO'
_____
= WEAPON

_ _ _

_ _ _

_ _ _ _ _ _

117. LORD of THE RINGS

Which ring is linked with most rings?

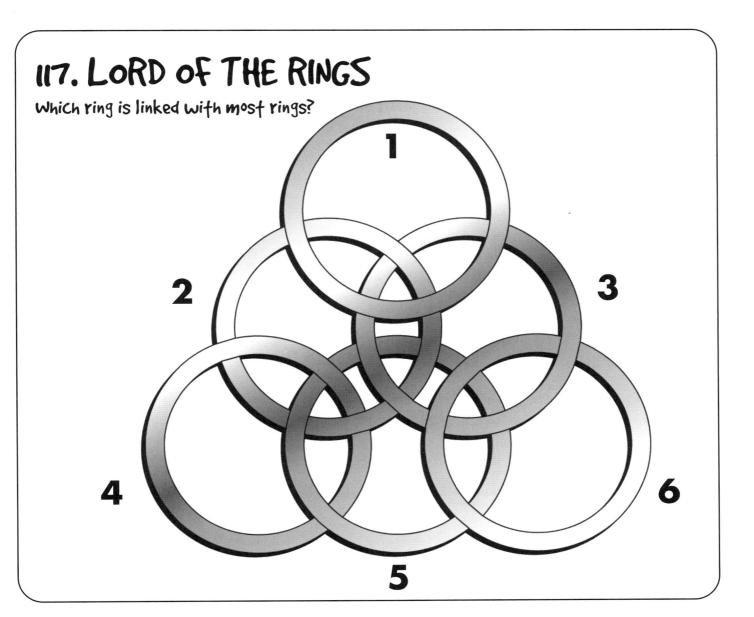

118. ALPHA VEG!

These vegetables have been chopped up and the letters arranged in alphabetical order. Can you work out what they all are?

1. A C O R R T _____
2. A O O P T T _____
3. O P R S T U _____
4. A C H I N P S _____
5. C E E L T T U _____

119. NUMBER BOX

Use all the numbers from 1 to 16 to fill in the spaces in the box. Each row across, each column down and each diagonal from corner to corner must contain FOUR numbers that add up to the same total.

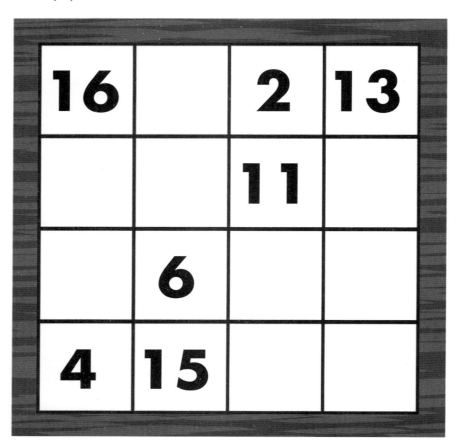

120. MORE OR LESS

What is more, the number of days in five weeks, or the number of eggs in three dozen?

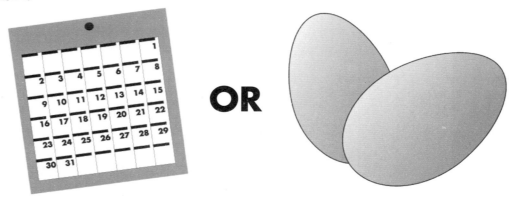

OR

121. MIND THE GAP

Which single three-letter word completes all of the following words?

O T _ _ _

R A S _ _ _ S

S P _ _ _ E

_ _ _ M I T

122. AFTER WORDS

Which word can go after all these words to make new words?

B A S K E T _____

B E A C H _____

F O O T _____

123. LINKS

Which word will go after the first word and before the second word?

S C R A M B L E D (_ _ _) W H I S K

124. TRIANGLES

Work out the number pattern then decide which number should appear inside the empty triangle.

15 **13** 2   15 **11** 4   15 **9** 6   15 / 8

125. SECRET SEVEN

Rearrange the letters in the word below to make another word of seven letters.

R E N T A L S

_ _ _ _ _ _ _

CLUE

Think
STAG'S HEAD

126. TOP TEN

complete the word by filling the spaces with a whole number between ONE and TEN.

6

5

NE___RKING

4

2   3   9   10

127. CHOCS AWAY

Select one of the numbered chocolates to go into the space in the box. The choc you choose must be different from all the others in the box. Which one is it?

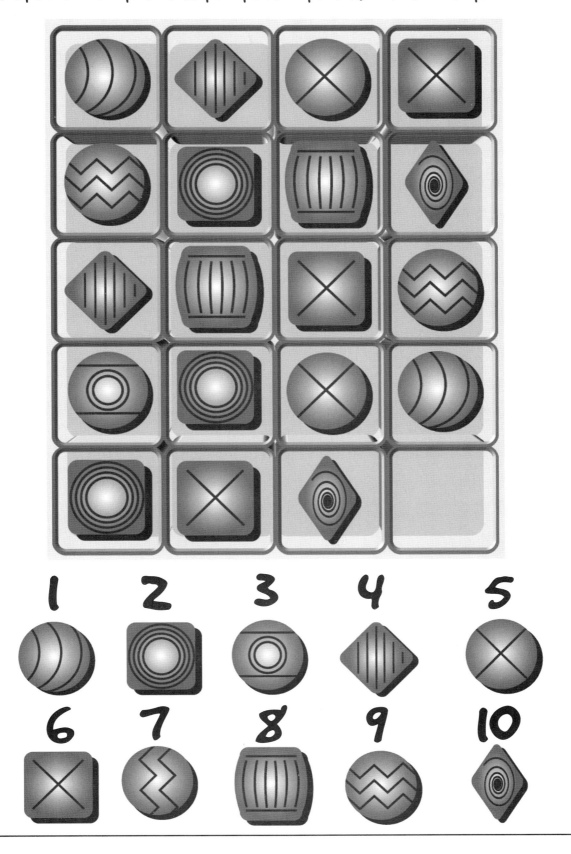

128. NUMBER RING

Starting from the top arrow and moving around the circle, can you work out the correct number to go in the empty section, to continue the number pattern?

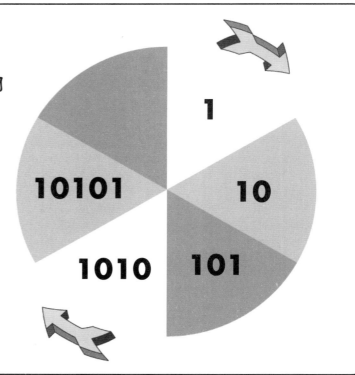

1

10

101

1010

10101

---

129. BACK WORDS

Solve the clues: the second answer is the first answer written backwards.

AT PRESENT   *   **DIDN'T LOSE**

*

___ ___ ___   ___ ___ ___

---

130. MIND THE GAP

Which single three-letter word completes all of the following words?

T R U _ _ _

_ _ _ L E

N A _ _ _

M A J E _ _ _

131. PEGGED IT!

There are nine tent pegs fixed in the ground. The picture shows the tent rope wound round four pegs to make a square. How many different squares can you make in total?

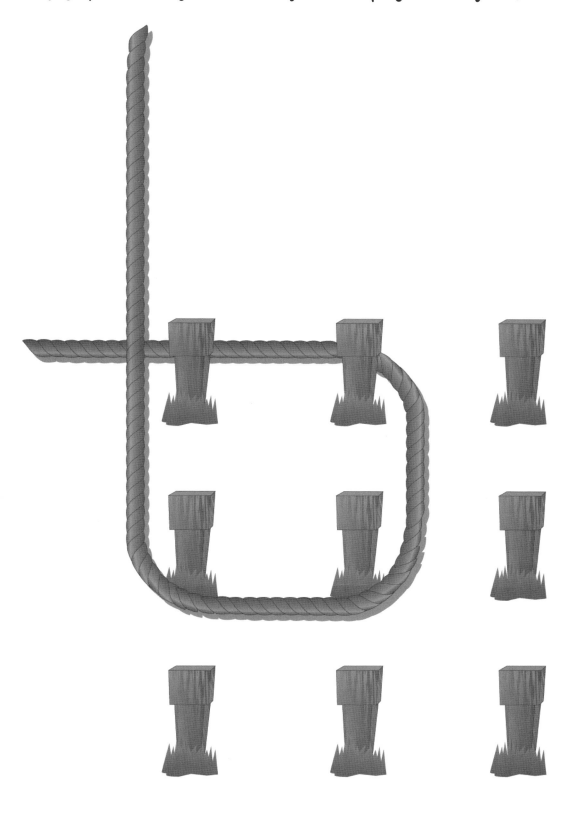

132. SEASHORE SEARCH

Search the seashore for the hidden words.

BOAT
CRAB
JELLYFISH
LILOS
ROCKPOOL
SANDCASTLE
SEAWEED
SHELLS
STARFISH
SURF
SWIMMERS
TIDES
WAVES

O	S	E	L	T	S	A	C	D	N	A	S
S	T	T	S	W	I	U	G	A	V	E	E
C	A	H	U	C	R	D	A	V	D	W	A
W	R	E	R	W	A	V	E	S	R	S	W
O	F	S	F	C	R	E	P	S	U	P	E
T	I	R	O	C	K	P	O	O	L	P	E
L	S	H	O	L	I	D	O	S	C	I	D
I	H	I	S	H	D	T	A	O	B	S	X
L	F	P	S	L	K	S	K	Y	A	I	U
O	S	W	I	M	M	E	R	S	R	E	T
S	H	E	L	L	S	F	I	V	C	S	P
M	A	J	H	S	I	F	Y	L	L	E	J

133. WHO'S THERE?

Here's the name of an animal, but any vowel letters - that's A, E, I, O and U - have been taken out. Can you tell what it is?

L P H N T

134. ADDER

Using other words with the same meaning,
can you create a new word from two separate ones?

   BABY'S BED   _ _ _

+ HEAVY WEIGHT   _ _ _

= FABRIC   _ _ _ _ _ _

---

135. NUMBER SEARCH

Try and search out these numbers in the grid! The numbers
always go in a straight line.

```
2 5 0 5 2 4 0 3 7 0 2 2
1 1 3 6 8 7 5 5 0 4 1 5
6 5 3 5 7 4 2 4 5 0 4 9
6 2 2 5 2 7 5 2 9 0 5 8
1 9 1 3 0 5 2 8 0 4 9 7
5 6 8 5 1 8 6 1 4 5 4 7
4 6 8 8 1 7 4 8 6 3 2 6
4 0 8 5 0 4 1 5 3 5 0 5
1 9 5 8 5 5 4 1 9 0 9 4
0 5 0 8 1 8 1 2 4 9 0 5
3 8 9 5 4 9 0 4 5 4 9 3
1 5 6 9 0 6 3 3 1 2 3 0
```

11368	
12330	
18080	
19130	
20110	
21661	
27220	
29660	
31230	
31711	
37022	
41410	
44103	
68901	
69063	
77216	
81812	
83003	
94209	
98776	

136. AFTER WORDS
Which word can go after all these words to make new words?

NEWS _____

WRITING _____

NOTE _____

137. FACE IT
What is the total of all the numbers that make up the face?

138. PAIRS

Pair the six listed words together so that three new words are formed.

GO
HAT
HER
MAN
PANT
RED

① _____

② _____

③ _____

139. TOP TEN

Complete the word by filling the spaces with a whole number between ONE and TEN.

4 3 2   L _ _ _ S O M E   9 1 5

140. BACK WORDS

Solve the clues: the second answer is the first answer written backwards.

FRIEND   *   CIRCUIT IN A RACE

___ ___ ___ ___   *   ___ ___ ___ ___

141. SWEET TREATS

See how many things you can find in the shop.

I	S	I	R	S	N	I	F	F	U	M	S
E	T	L	G	H	D	C	E	J	A	J	M
X	I	H	L	O	V	E	L	K	E	O	I
S	U	A	R	O	O	Z	Q	I	T	Y	R
S	C	O	N	E	R	R	X	J	A	C	G
E	S	U	M	M	E	R	I	N	G	U	E
I	I	N	J	A	M	T	R	F	B	P	P
R	B	P	R	L	C	R	I	A	L	C	E
T	M	A	C	L	V	I	G	H	D	A	S
S	T	E	H	O	A	F	D	W	G	K	N
A	T	E	A	W	M	L	T	E	Y	E	D
P	T	A	E	S	F	E	R	B	E	U	I

BISCUITS   **GATEAU**   **PASTRIES**

CUPCAKE   **MALLOWS**   **ROLLS**

ECLAIR   **MERINGUE**   **SCONE**

FLAN   **MUFFINS**   **TRIFLE**

142. LINKS
Which word will go after the first word and before the second word?

F I E L D (_ _ _ _ _) M A T

143. SECRET SEVEN
Rearrange the letters in the word below to make another word of seven letters.

S T R A I T S

_ _ _ _ _ _ _

CLUE

Think
PAINTERS

144. MIND THE GAP
Which single three-letter word completes all of the following words?

C L A R I _ _ _

_ _ _ T L E

N I _ _ _ Y

C A S T A _ _ _ S

1. PAINT BOX

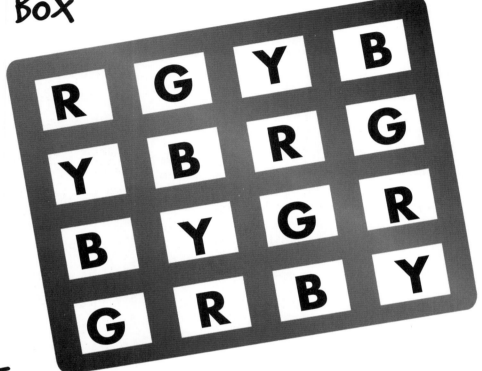

2. LINKS

Sand.

3. CLOCKWORK

Clock B. The time would be 8.35.

4. CREATURE CODE

1. Bear   2. Zebra   3. Rabbit   4. Tiger.

5. BIRTHDAY

May is the birthday girl.

Her friends are April and June.

6. TOP TEN

one. This completes the word honest.

7. ADDER

Bar + Row = Barrow.

8. UNWANTED

The unused word is YOU.

9. PIC-TRICK

Imp.

10. SECRET SEVEN

Actress.

11. CASUALTY!

A. Matt first

B. Ally last

C. Pete second

D. Michelle third.

12. MORE OR LESS
They are both the same – 30.

13. EYE CHART
1. A
2. Am
3. Man
4. Moan
5. Roman
6. Maroon

14. LINK LETTERS
The missing letters spell PANEL.

15. SPLITZER
Flute, organ.

16. STAR GAZING
Star group 1.

17. AFTER WORDS
House.

18. JUST THE JOB
Nurse, Cook, Teacher, Doctor, Vet.

19. NUMBER RING
5. Each number is halved with every move.

20. SECRET SEVEN
Redhead.

21. LINKS

Tennis.

22. TRI-TANGLE

16.

23. TOP TEN

Ten. This completes the word content.

24. FIRST CHANGE

1. Ball/Call   2. Mow/Now   3. Fame/Game   4. Line/Mine   5. Round/Sound.

25. TWO TIMER

Time is hidden twice.

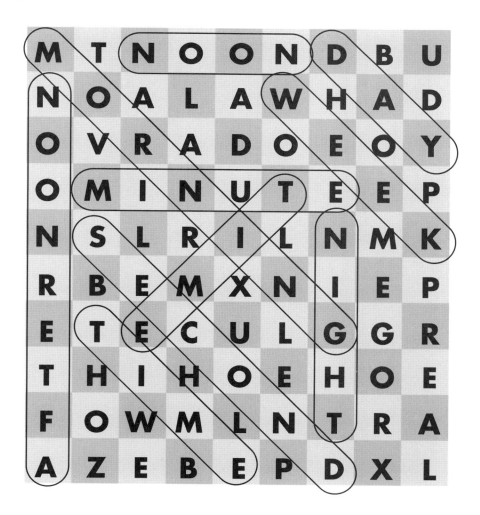

26. ADDER

Arm + our = Armour.

27. MAZE CRAZE

Beware of crazy mazes!

28. BACK WORDS

Gel * Leg.

29. CUBED

C	U	B	E
U	G	L	Y
B	L	U	E
E	Y	E	S

S	C	A	R
C	U	B	E
A	B	L	E
R	E	E	K

30. REALLY WILD!

1. Bear
2. Lion
3. Snake
4. Tiger
5. Zebra
6. Elephant.

31. WHAT AM I?

Secret.

32. LINE-NINE

Move the lines as shown. There are now four triangles of the same size and the outer lines of the pattern form a further triangle.

33. MIND THE GAP

Eat.

34. HIT LIST

8 hits on day one. 14 on day two.
20 on day three. 26 on day four. 32 on day five.

35. AFTER WORDS

Room.

36 .BRUSHSTROKES

A, G, E, C, D, B, F.

37. SECRET SEVEN

Married.

38. HALF TIME

1. Core
2. Rest
3. Stir
4. Iris
5. Isle
6. Lead
7. Adam.

39. COUNTER-FIT

Take the second counter and place it over the bottom left counter in the corner.

40. LINKS

Ball.

41. LOCKER ROOM

Locker number 14.

42. SPLIT UP

1. d
2. e
3. a
4. b
5. f
6. c.

43. BACK WORDS

Dam * Mad.

44. FRUIT MACHINE

Grapes,
Cherries,
Banana.

45. ADDER

Ant + Hem = Anthem.

46. VOWEL PLAY

1. London
2. Paris
3. Tokyo
4. Dublin
5. Oslo.

47. SIDEWAYS

Both equal 48.

48. SECRET SEVEN

Starved.

49. JOBSWORTH

1. Nurse
2. Tutor
3. Warden
4. Mason
5. Teacher.

50. ROWS AND ARROWS

Start

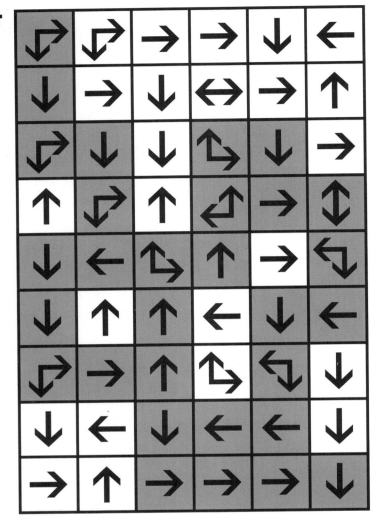

Finish

51. SPLITZER

Panda, Tiger.

52. WINNERS

1. Wind   2. Wings   3. Window

4. Winks   5. Wine.

53. CHILL OUT

1. Heat   2. Head   3. Held

4. Hold   5. Cold

54. NUMBER TRAIL

Line B.

55. AFTER WORDS

Time.

56. TIME TURN

1. Time
2. Tame
3. Same
4. Some
5. Sole
6. Sale
7. Tale
8. Tile.

57. TOM'S TASTES

Tom likes fruits which are also the names of colours.

58. SECRET SEVEN

Altered.

59. HORSE CODE

What does a horse call a bad dream?
A nightmare!

60. PIC-TRICK

Lost in space.

61. BACK WORDS

Bin * Nib.

62. SHADY

1. Codes
2. Daisy
3. Paste
4. Mikes
5. Modem
6. Error
7. Print
8. Saved
9. Treat. The shaded letters spell Diskdrive.

63. WORLD TOUR

1. Iran 2. Israel 3. China 4. Laos 5. Greenland.

64. NEW IDEAS

I	D	E	A
D	E	A	R
E	A	S	T
A	R	T	S

P	I	N	E
I	D	E	A
N	E	S	T
E	A	T	S

T	R	I	P
R	O	D	E
I	D	E	A
P	E	A	R

65. MIND THE GAP

Pen.

66. ADDER

Solution: Ash + ore = Ashore.

67. INVISIBLE COLOUR

Red.

68. NUMBER-RING

22. 1 is added to the first number, 2 to the second, 3 to the third, 4 to the fourth and five to the fifth.

69. AFTER WORDS

Book.

70. INSTRUMENTAL

1. Horn
2. Drum
3. Cello
4. Organ
5. Piano.

71. TOP TEN

Two. This completes the word Artwork.

72. SPLITZER

Lunch, Snack.

73. BACK WORDS

Wed * Dew.

74. SAIL AWAY

Sails on yacht 3. Each section of pattern moves one position round the sails in a clockwise direction.

75. LINKS

Butter.

76. CODED NUMBERS

1. Ten
2. Twenty
3. Two
4. Nineteen.

77. MORE OR LESS

The number of years in a century: 100 against 96.

78. WRITING ON THE WALL

1. Mummy
2. Pyramids
3. Tomb
4. Camel
5. Desert.

79. SECRET SEVEN

Gallery.

80. CONNECTING ROOMS

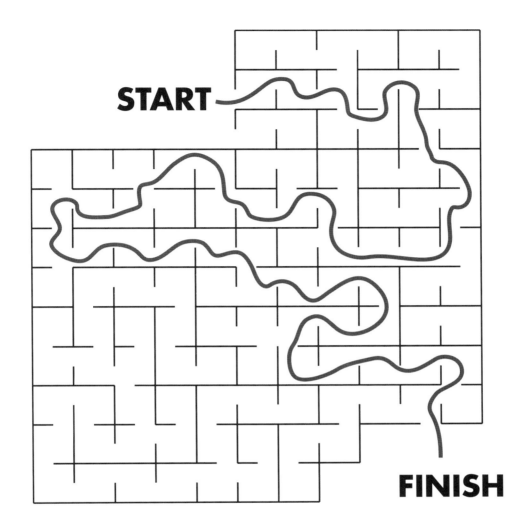

START

FINISH

81. CALENDAR COUNT

The number of days in January and December, 62, is greater than the number of months in five years, 60.

82. GO FOURTH

ENDS. Each group makes a word square. If the words are written in rows, the columns reading down will form the same words as those when reading across.

83. AFTER WORDS

Moon.

84. NUMBER RING

243. Each number is multiplied by 3.

3 x 81 = 243.

85. FOOT FIND

1. Shoe
2. Slipper
3. Sandal.

86. TOP TEN

Ten. This completes the word attention.

87. ADDER

Boo + Tee = Bootee.

88. FRUIT FRIENDS

Geena: orange.

Lizzie: Lime.

Neil: Melon.

Paula: Grapefruit.

Peter: Tangerine.

89. BACK WORDS

Nip * Pin.

90. SQUARE EYES

Eight squares in all.

91. LINKS

Alarm.

92. PICK A CARD

Left to right: five of hearts, ten of clubs, three of spades and two of diamonds.

93. SECRET SEVEN

Earring.

94. BREAKER

1. d
2. e
3. a
4. b
5. c.

95. MIND THE GAP

Mat.

96. COMET CODE

1. Comet
2. Moon
3. Meteor.

97. SPLITZER

China, Egypt.

98. TON UP

4, 25, 31, 9, 17, 14.

99. LADDER

Tenth, Tench, Teach, Peach, Peace, Place.

100. TIME TOTAL

Both are equal, at 150.

101. ADDER

Car + Rot = carrot.

102. KID'S STUFF

1. Kid
2. Cub
3. Lamb
4. Pup.

103. STRANGE SUM

X = 7,
Y = 4,
Z = 9.
497 + 447 = 944.

104. MIND THE GAP

Tar.

105. AFTER WORDS

Hound.

106. TOP TEN

one. This completes the word done.

107. TIME TWISTER

1. Day
2. Hour
3. Week
4. Second
5. Minute.

108. TV SALES

A2,
C3,
D3.

109. SECRET SEVEN

Answers.

110. PLAY THE SYMBOLS

1. Triangle
2. Piano
3. organ
4. Guitar.

111. BACK WORDS

Net * Ten.

112. LINKS

Milk.

113. DOCTOR, DOCTOR!

The London doctor was his sister.

114. SPLITZER

Radio,

Video.

115. DAYS MAZE

The number of days in June, July and August total 92,
the days in September, October and November total 91.

116. ADDER

Can + Non = Cannon.

117. LORD OF THE RINGS

Ring number 2.

118. ALPHA VEG!

1. Carrot
2. Potato
3. Sprout
4. Spinach
5. Lettuce

119. NUMBER BOX

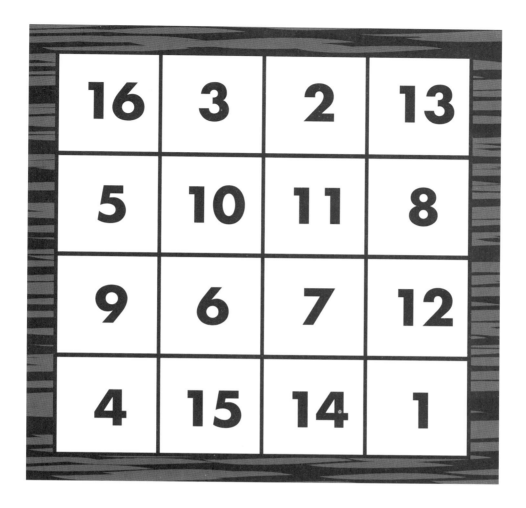

16	3	2	13
5	10	11	8
9	6	7	12
4	15	14	1

120. MORE OR LESS

The number of eggs in three dozen, 36, is more than the days in five weeks, which is 35.

121. MIND THE GAP

Her.

122. AFTER WORDS

Ball.

123. LINKS

Egg.

124. TRIANGLES

7. The number inside the triangle plus the number on the right add up to the number on the left.

125. SECRET SEVEN

Antlers.

126. TOP TEN

Two. This completes the word networking.

127. CHOCS AWAY

Chocolate number 7.

128. NUMBER-RING

101010. First an 'o' then an 'I' is added to the end of the previous numbers.

129. BACK WORDS

Now * Won.

130. MIND THE GAP

Sty.

131. PEGGED IT!

Six squares can be made. Four small squares can be made, as shown. A fifth can be made going round all the pegs. A sixth is made by going round the middle four pegs on the outside edge of the pattern.

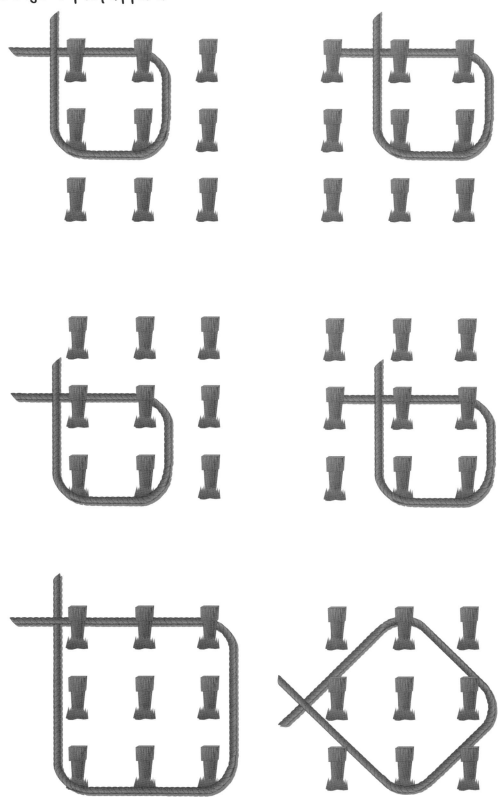

132. SEASHORE SEARCH

O	S	E	L	T	S	A	C	D	N	A	S
S	T	T	S	W	I	U	G	A	V	E	E
C	A	H	U	C	R	D	A	V	D	W	A
W	R	E	R	W	A	V	E	S	R	S	W
O	F	S	F	C	R	E	P	S	U	P	E
T		R	O	C	K	P	O	O	L	P	E
I	S	H	O	L	I	D	O	S	C	I	D
H	I	S	H	D	T	A	O	B	S	X	
L	F	P	S	L	K	S	K	Y	A	I	U
O	S	W	I	M	M	E	R	S	R	E	T
S	H	E	L	L	S	F	I	V	C	S	P
M	A	J	H	S	I	F	Y	L	L	E	J

133. WHO'S THERE?

Elephant.

134. ADDER

Cot + Ton = cotton.

135. NUMBER SEARCH

2	5	0	5	2	4	0	3	7	0	2	2
1	1	3	6	8	7	5	5	0	4	1	5
6	5	3	5	7	4	2	4	5	0	4	9
6	2	2	5	2	7	5	2	9	0	5	8
1	9	1	3	0	5	2	8	0	4	9	7
5	6	8	5	1	8	6	1	4	5	4	7
4	6	8	8	1	7	4	8	6	3	2	6
4	0	8	5	0	4	1	5	3	5	0	5
1	9	5	8	5	5	4	1	9	0	9	4
0	5	0	8	1	8	1	2	4	9	0	5
3	8	9	5	4	9	0	4	5	4	9	3
1	5	6	9	0	6	3	3	1	2	3	0

136. AFTER WORDS

Paper.

137. FACE IT

The total is 26:

Face = 0,

Eyes = 8,

Nose = 2,

Eyebrows = 3,

Mouth = 1,

Ears = 6 (x2).

138. PAIRS

Hatred,

Mango,

Panther.

139. TOP TEN

one. This completes the word lonesome.

140. BACK WORDS

Pal * Lap.

141. SWEET TREATS

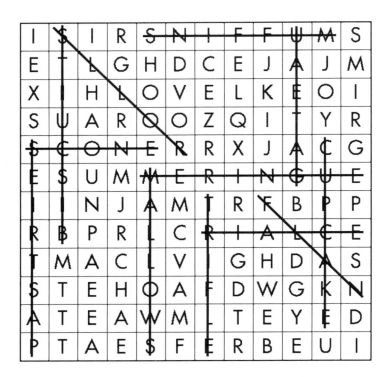

I	S	I	R	S	N	I	F	F	U	M	S
E	T	L	G	H	D	C	E	J	A	J	M
X	I	H	L	O	V	E	L	K	E	O	I
S	U	A	R	O	O	Z	Q	I	T	Y	R
S	C	O	N	E	R	R	X	J	A	C	G
E	S	U	M	M	E	R	I	N	G	U	E
I	I	N	J	A	M	T	R	T	B	P	P
R	B	P	R	L	C	R	I	A	L	C	E
T	M	A	C	L	V	G	H	D	A	S
S	T	E	H	O	A	F	D	W	G	K	N
A	T	E	A	W	M	L	T	E	Y	F	D
P	T	A	E	S	F	E	R	B	E	U	I

142. LINKS
Mouse.

143. SECRET SEVEN
Artists.

144. MIND THE GAP
Net.

LEVEL TWO QUESTIONS

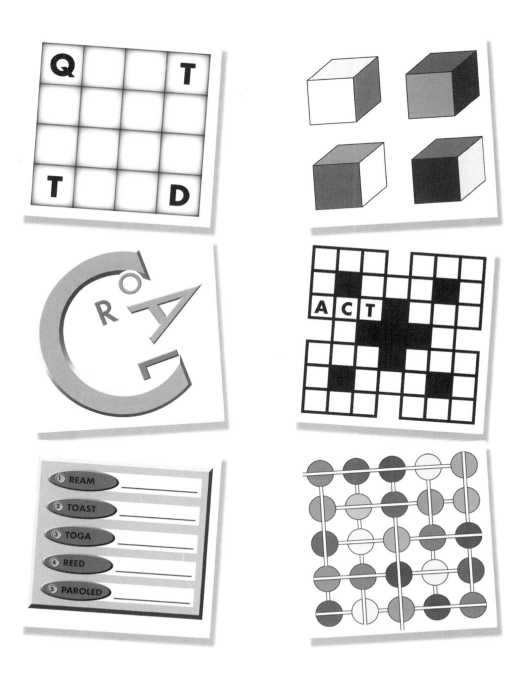

1. MOSAIC

Fit the letter tiles back into the frame. When the tiles fit together in the right order, the mosaic has FIVE words reading across, and FOUR words reading down.

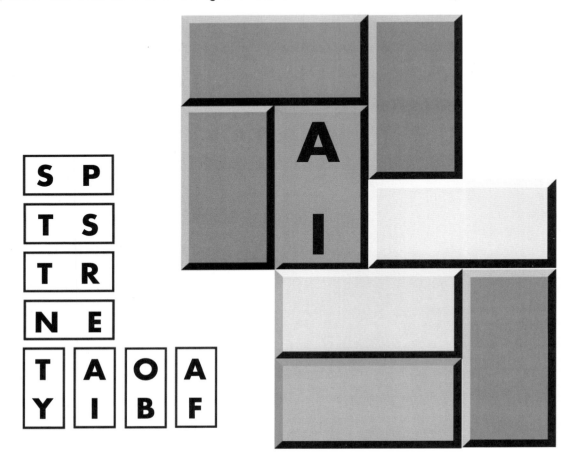

S	P
T	S
T	R
N	E
T			
Y	A	O	A
	I	B	F

2. AFTER-WORDS

Which word can go after all these words to make new words?

F R I E N D —————————————

S P A C E —————————————

W A R —————————————

3. BEEP BEEP!

Emma's new watch gives an amazingly loud beep every time that a 3 appears. Each minute a new set of four digits is displayed. If two 3s appear at the same time there would be two beeps and if three 3s appeared there would be three beeps.

(If four 3s appeared it would be time to get a new watch, as the time would be 33.33!)

How many beeps will there be between 08.00 and 09.00?

4. OFF LINE

Remove three lines to be left with a pattern of exactly FOUR squares.

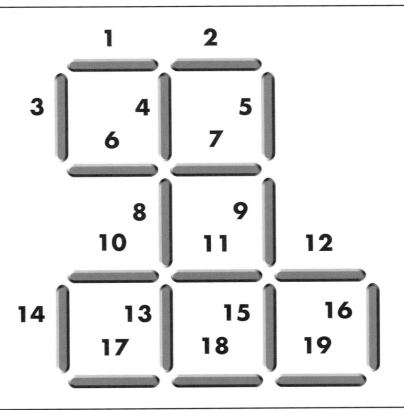

5. ON GUARD

Find a way through the passageway without coming across a guard (shown as circles).

6. SECRET SEVEN

Rearrange the letters in the word below to make another word of seven letters.

A S S U A G E

CLUE

Think HOT DOG

7. BRUSH STROKES

How many brushes are pictured here?

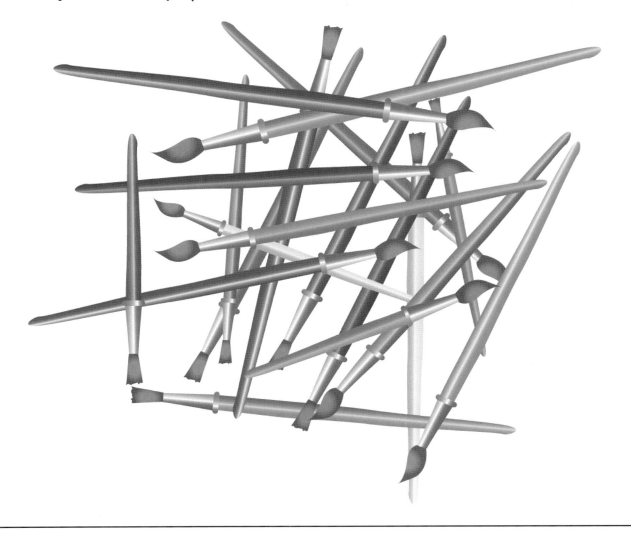

8. MIND THE GAP

Which single three-letter word completes all of the following words?

C _ _ _ I N G

R E C _ _ _ _

_ _ _ _ O C A T E

G _ _ _ E R Y

9. QUARTERBACK

A word square reads the same across and down. Fit the listed words back to make four word squares, each containing four words. One word is in position to start you off.

AVOW
DARK
DELL
EVIL
HIVE
IDEA
KIND
LOVE
NEAR
OGRE
PEEK
PEWS
SHED
SLAP
SOUP
URGE

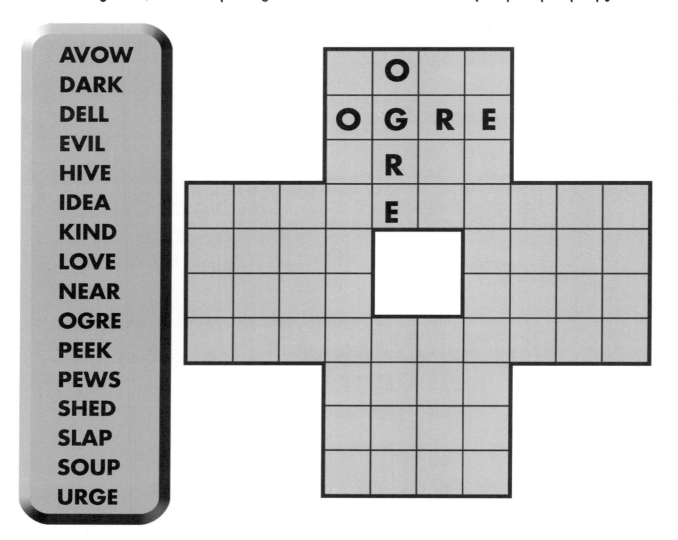

10. SPLITZER

Split this row of ten letters into two five-letter words which are the names of body organs. The words read from left to right and the letters are in the correct order.

H L E I A V R E R T

11. TRIANGLE TEST

How many triangles are in this pattern?

12. HONEYCOMB

Each answer contains six letters and is written in the six spaces that link together around a number. Answers always go in a clockwise direction and every first letter is in place. When the honeycomb is complete the inner ring of six letters will spell out a star sign.

1 Old fashioned sea bandit.

2 People protecting or watching over a place.

3 Rough and tough.

4 Unlawful killing.

5 Season of the year.

6 Metal fastening bolts.

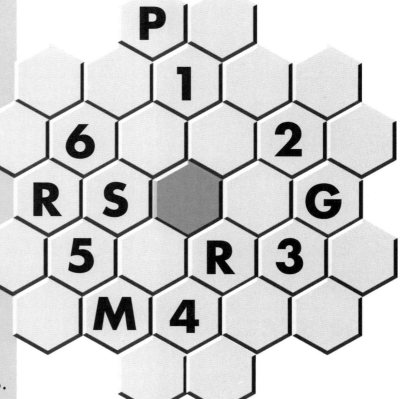

13. BACK WORDS

Solve the clues: the second answer is the first answer written backwards.

GIVE MONEY * HIGH-PITCHED BARK

*

14. MORE OR LESS

Which is greater, the number of hours in three days, or the number of eggs in five and a half dozen?

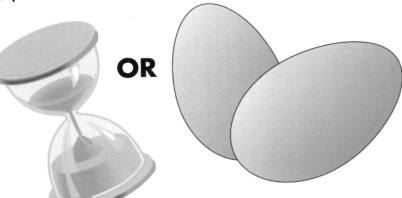

OR

15. ADDER

Using other words with the same meaning, can you create a new word from two separate ones?

ORGAN OF HEARING   _ _ _

+ FALSE HAIR   _ _ _
_____
= INSECT   _ _ _ _ _ _

16. CREATURE CODE

In this code, symbols have been used to take the place of letters of the alphabet. The first group spells out the word RAT. Can you work out the other coded creatures?

1 ✳ ✡ ✳   R A T

2 ☆ ✡ ✳ ✳ ☆ ✳

3 ☆ ✡ ★ ♣ ✡

✡	✢	✣	✤	✥	◆	◇	★	☆	✪	✩	✦	✶
A	B	C	D	E	F	G	H	I	J	K	L	M

✯	✬	✫	✳	✺	✴	✶	✴	✷	✸	✹	❄
N	O	P	Q	R	S	T	U	V	W	X	Y	Z

---

17. LINKS

Which word will go after the first word and before the second word?

A I R _ _ _ _ _ H O L E

---

18. SECRET SEVEN

Rearrange the letters in the word below to make another word of seven letters.

B A N T A M S

_ _ _ _ _ _ _

CLUE

Think SPORTS MAN

19. PICTURE GALLERY

Use the clues to find the portrait of Sir Jasper Murgatroyd.

- Sir Jasper has a moustache.
- Sir Jasper wears a hat.
- Sir Jasper has a beard.
- Sir Jasper has a scar on his left cheek.
- Sir Jasper has large, bushy eyebrows.

1

2

3

4

5

20. GIVE ME FIVE

Solve the clues, so that each answer contains five letters. Write all the answers in place and the shaded squares reading down will reveal the name of a musical instrument.

1. Opposite of last
2. Outer covering of an egg
3. Sailing boat
4. Bad weather
5. Portable light
6. Push this to power a bicycle
7. Meadow
8. Number in a trio

1				
2				
3				
4				
5				
6				
7				
8				

21. CARD TRICK

How do you turn pans into a card game?

_____

22. LOTS of SPOTS

Using the words listed, make three word squares which read the same across and down. The word SPOT appears in each square.

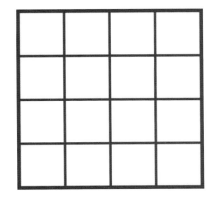
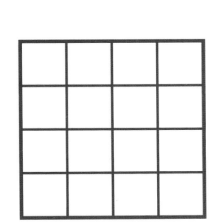
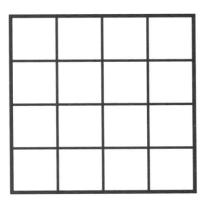

DODO, DROP, ETNA, ISLE, LOAN, ODDS, OVAL, PAVE, SPOT, SPOT, SPOT, TELL

23. TOP TEN

complete the word by filling the spaces with a whole number between ONE and TEN.

E X _ _ _ D

24. WHAT'S NEXT?

What is the next letter to go in the space?

25. ANIMAL FILL

Think of the name of a creature that will fill in the spaces and complete the name of another creature.

P _ _ _ H E R

26. TREE SURGERY

Can you unscramble the groups of letters to spell out different parts of a tree?

1. **RAKB** _____

2. **SORTO** _____

3. **RANCHB** _____

4. **FALE** _____

5. **TNRUK** _____

27. SPLITZER

Split this row of ten letters into two five-letter words which are the names of birds. The words read from left to right and the letters are in the correct order.

E G A G L O O E S E

_____ / _____

28. BLOCKS

Can you fit the blocks below into the grid to read the message?

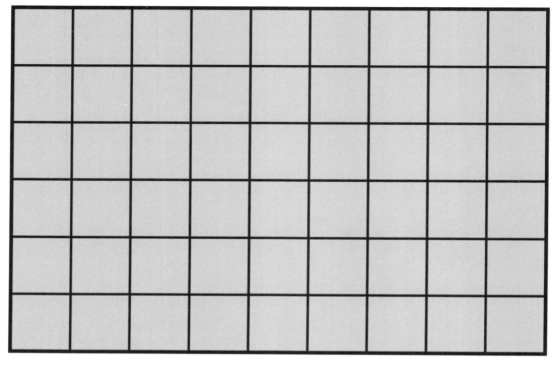

T	H	A
T	E	N
F	O	R

	T	H
	C	K	S
		F	R

P	U	T
B	L	O
T	H	E

E	S	E
	I	N
A	M	E

S	O	
S	E	N
I	S	

T		A
C	E	
M	E	D

29. ON LINE

Add one line to complete each letter and spell out a high tech item.

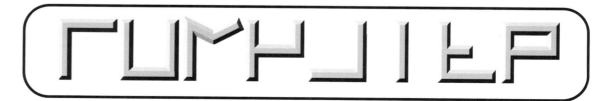

30. NICE MICE

Solve each clue and write the answers into the spaces in the grid. All answers have four letters. Put the first letter in the outer circle, then move towards the centre. Only one letter changes between answers, and answer 8 will be only one letter different from answer 1.

1 Scurrying creatures.
2 Food often eaten with a Chinese meal.
3 Speed contest.
4 Part of the body with nose, eyes and mouth.
5 Price for a ticket to travel.
6 Flames and smoke.
7 A folder in which to keep papers.
8 Measure of distance.

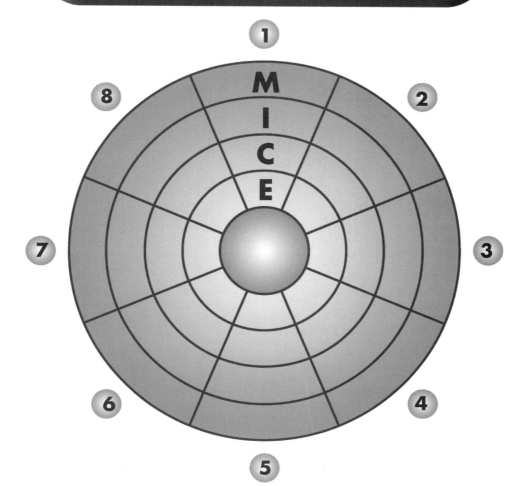

31. LINKS
Which word will go after the first word and before the second word?

B L U E _ _ _ _ _ S H A R K

32. ON TARGET
Which three numbers will have to be hit to make exactly 80?

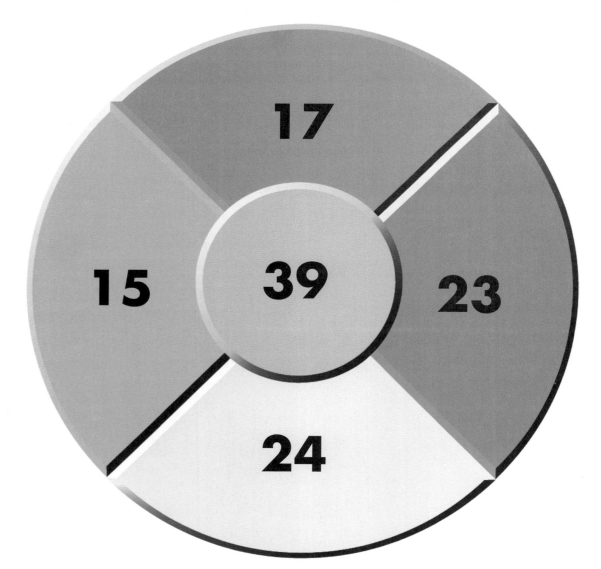

33. AFTER WORDS

Which word can go after all these words to make new words?

D E A D _____

L I F E _____

O N _____

34. NUMBER-RING

Move around the circle. You have to write a number in the blank section that will continue the number pattern.

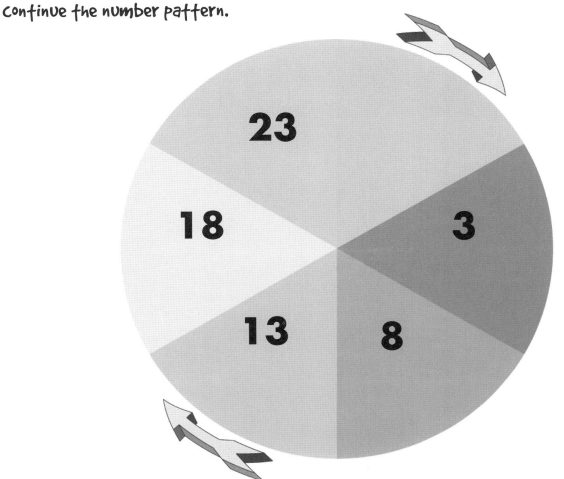

35. SECRET SEVEN

Rearrange the letters in the word below to make another word of seven letters.

B O R E D O M

_ _ _ _ _ _ _

CLUE
Think
IN THE HOUSE

36. PAIRS

Which two badges are exactly alike?

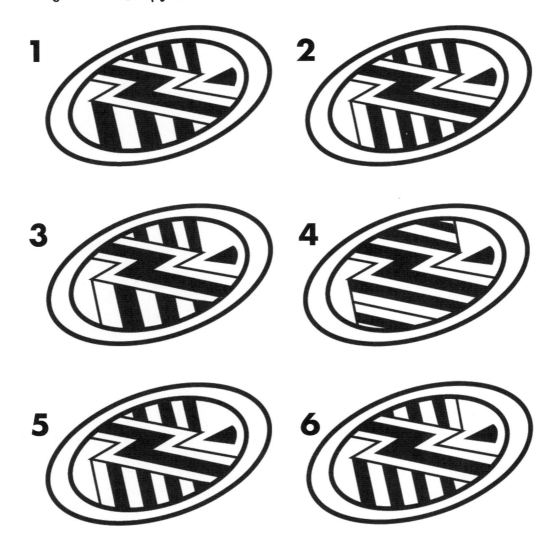

37. MIND THE GAP

Which single three-letter word completes all of the following words?

D E _ _ _ E

_ _ _ C H

_ _ _ T E R Y

_ _ _ T L E

38. MORE OR LESS

What is more, the number of sides in nine triangles, or the number of sides in four octagons?

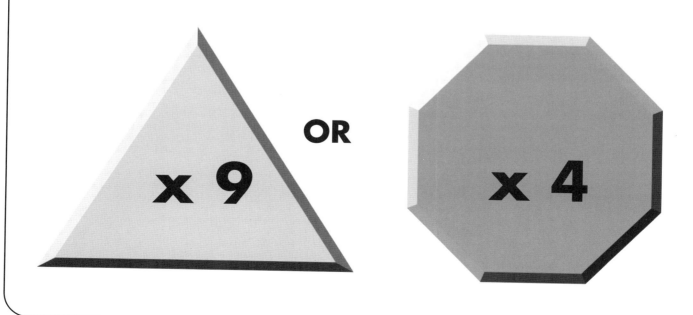

x 9   OR   x 4

39. BACK WORDS

Solve the clues: the second answer is the first answer written backwards.

HOLE IN THE GROUND * UPPER EDGE

___ ___ ___ ___   *   ___ ___ ___ ___

40. SNAKES ALIVE!

The name of a type of snake is hidden in each of the sentences below. Find them by joining words or parts of words together.

1 How sad Derek looks.

2 They stayed all night at their daughter's disco, bravely in my opinion.

3 The Jumbo arrived on time.

41. SPIDER'S WEB

Which spider's web trail leads to the centre of the web?

42. NATIONWIDE

Rearrange the letters in the words below to spell out the names of countries.

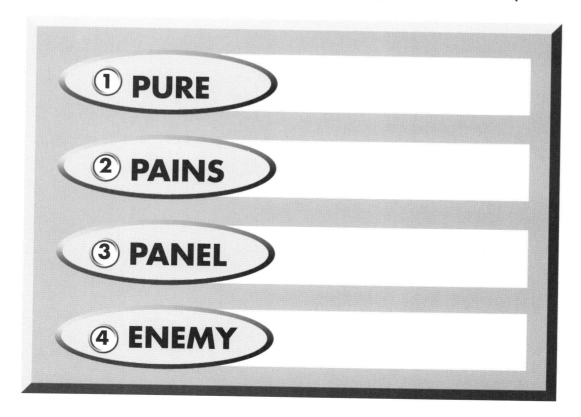

① PURE

② PAINS

③ PANEL

④ ENEMY

43. ADDER

Using other words with the same meaning, can you create a new word from two separate ones?

LIMB

+ FINISH

_ _ _
_ _ _

─────────────────

= OLD STORY

_ _ _ _ _ _

44. FACE FACTS

Use the letters that make up the face to make a name.

45. SECRET SEVEN

Rearrange the letters in the word below to make another word of seven letters.

B O L S T E R

_ _ _ _ _ _ _

CLUE

Think SHELLFISH

46. OWL SIGNS

Shapes and signs have been used to take the place of letters of the alphabet. Can you work out what the words are? They are all creatures and the first word is OWL.

1 ★ ✹ ✵

2 ✴ ★ ✵ ◆

3 ◆ ★ ✡ ✵

4 ◆ ★ ✴

OWL

_____

_____

_____

✡	✛	✜	♣	✛	◆	✦	★	☆	✪	✫	✯	✰
A	B	C	D	E	F	G	H	I	J	K	L	M

✩	✬	☆	✳	✴	✶	✷	✸	✦	✴	✴	✹	✺
N	O	P	Q	R	S	T	U	V	W	X	Y	Z

47. MIND THE GAP

Which single three-letter word completes all of the following words?

O _ _ _

_ _ _ _ A C E

A P _ _ _ L I N G

48. LINKS

Which word will go after the first word and before the second word?

R A I N _ _ _ T I E

49. BACK WORDS

Solve the clues: the second answer is the first answer written backwards.

PAN   *   SUMMIT

_ _ _   *   _ _ _

50. ON THE MAP

Here are four sketch maps of this scene. only one is correct in every detail.
Which one is it?

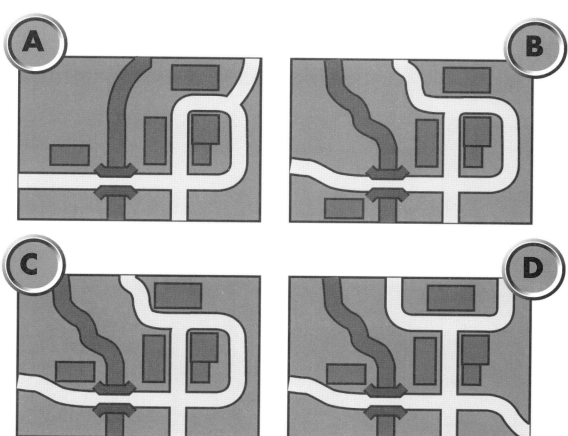

51. SQUASHED SANDWICHES!

Can you unscramble the groups of letters to spell out the names of sandwich fillings?

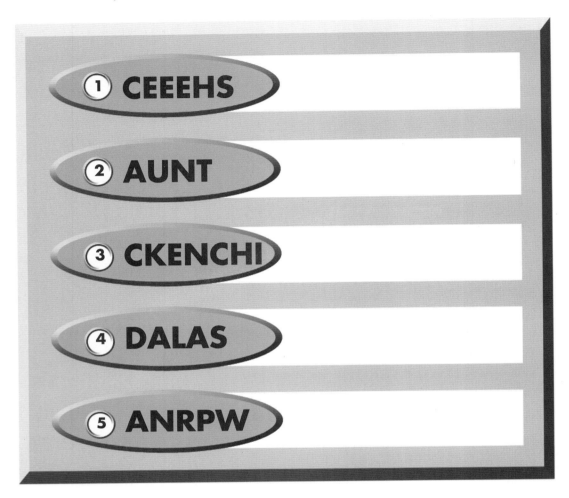

1. CEEEHS
2. AUNT
3. CKENCHI
4. DALAS
5. ANRPW

52. SECRET SEVEN

Rearrange the letters in the word below to make another word of seven letters.

P R E C A S T

CLUE

Think
FLOOR COVERINGS

53. 3D

With three Ds in place, can you fit all these three-letter words back into the frame?

AGE ALL ASH ASP AXE BAD

BOA DOE DUO DYE ELF END

FOX GNU HUT LID OFF OWL

POT YES

54. PATTERN PLAY
Which pattern is the odd one out?

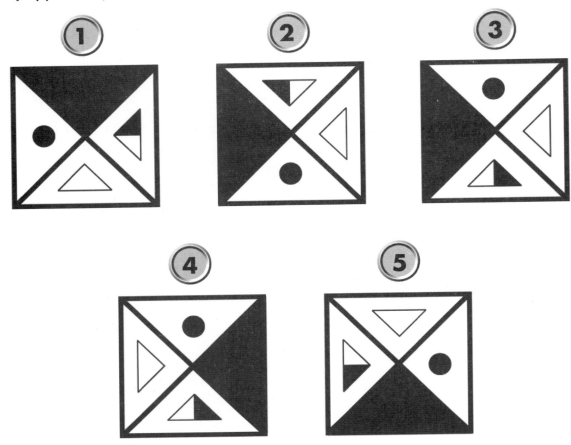

55. ADDER
Using other words with the same meaning, can you create a new word from two separate ones?

OVERWEIGHT
+ NOT HIM
_ _ _
_ _ _

= DAD
_ _ _ _ _

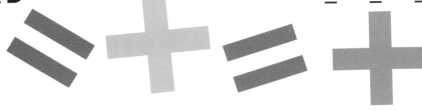

56. STARGAZER

All answers contain four letters and follow the direction shown by the arrows.

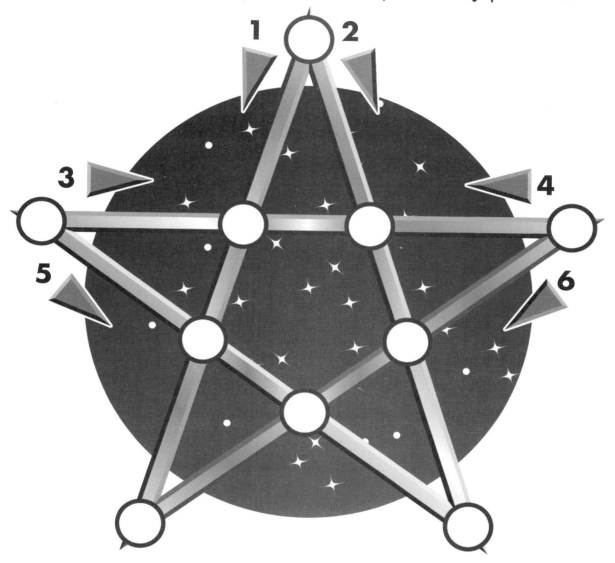

1. Pastry containing sweet or savoury filling
2. Light froth on the surface of a liquid
3. The movement of water
4. Wild dog-like animal
5. Place where crops are grown
6. Give notice of danger

57. COMPUTER CODE

Shapes and signs have been used to take the place of letters of the alphabet. The first group of symbols stands for the word COMPUTER. What computer-linked word does the second group make?

✡	✢	✣	✤	✥	◆	◇	★	☆	★	☆	☆	★
A	B	C	D	E	F	G	H	I	J	K	L	M

★	☆	☆	✱	✲	✳	✴	✷	★	✦	★	✹	✺
N	O	P	Q	R	S	T	U	V	W	X	Y	Z

58. MIND THE GAP

Which single three-letter word completes all of the following words?

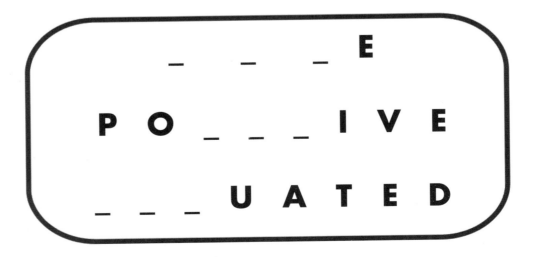

_ _ _ E

PO _ _ _ IVE

_ _ _ UATED

59. LEMON-AID

How many times does the word LEMON appear in the box of letters? It can read in any direction as a straight line of letters.

60. AFTER WORDS

Which word can go after all these words to make new words?

CODE _____

CROSS _____

PASS _____

61. ROUNDABOUT
Find a pathway that leads to the centre of the maze.

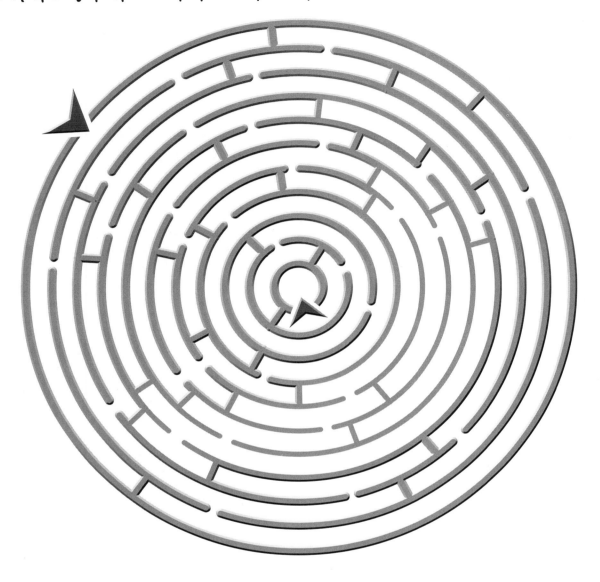

62. LINKS
Which word will go after the first word and before the second word?

T R E A S U R E _ _ _ _ _ _ N U T

63. CAPITAL, CAPITAL

The name of a capital city is hidden in each of the sentences below. Find them by joining words or parts of words together.

1 She gets mad riding behind slow moving traffic.

2 Grandpa risked great danger during the war it seems.

3 Taking a deep breath ensures you're then ready for anything.

4 I took the toy from Emily and gave it to her sister.

5 I told my cousin Rebecca I rode my bicycle with the greatest care.

6 The number line dancing has increased out of all proportion.

64. FRUITY

Take half of a PEAR.

Add the middle of a GRAPE.

Add one third of a CHERRY.

Which fruit have you got?

65. WHAT AM I?

My first is in stiff
But isn't in fish.

My second's in dash
But isn't in dish.

My third is in bread
But isn't in dear.

My fourth is in feel
But isn't in fear.

My fifth's not in fowl,
Though you'll find it in few.
You'll make the discovery
If you follow it through.

66. MORE OR LESS

What is more, the number of days in May doubled or the number of fortnights in two years?

OR

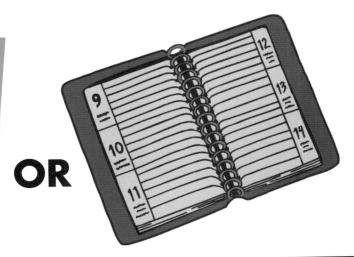

67. ALPHA NUMBERS

The groups of letters are arranged in alphabetical order. Move them round to spell out different numbers.

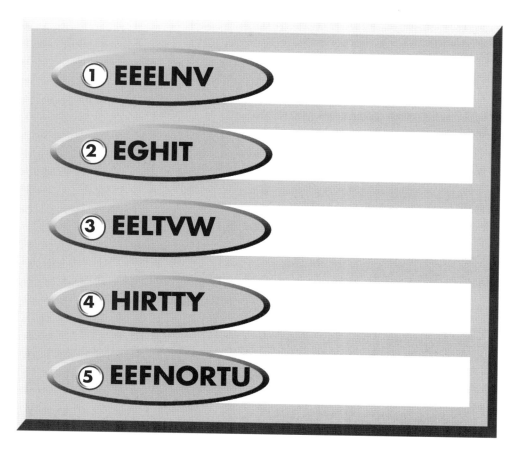

1. EEELNV
2. EGHIT
3. EELTVW
4. HIRTTY
5. EEFNORTU

68. SPLITZER

This row of ten letters can be split into two five-letter words which are the names of two types of boat. Words read from left to right and the letters are in the correct order. What are they?

C A Y A C N O H E T

/ _____

69. FAST TRACK

Four athletes have taken part in races. They have run different distances, and all finished in different positions. Can you work out each person's name, their event and finishing position?

70. BACK WORDS

Solve the clues: the second answer is the first answer written backwards.

RODENT * BLACK LIQUID

___ ___ ___ ___ * ___ ___ ___ ___

71. IN THE MIDDLE

Put a letter in each of the sets of brackets which can be added to the end of the first word and the start of the second word. The letters used will read down to spell out a fruit.

T O O (_) A N D
F A R (_) Y E S
F I R (_) E A T
H E R (_) P E N
S A W (_) E A R

72. YOUR DEAL

You have been dealt four playing cards that are all hearts.

The cards have consecutive numbers.

The four cards add up to 26.

Which cards have you been dealt?

73. COMPU-COMMAND

Add one line to complete each letter and spell out a computer command.

74. MOONS

Here are two moons. The first shows a moon against the night sky, the second shows a moon when it has been eclipsed so it appears as a dark object against a light sky. Which moon is the bigger of the two?

75. TOP TEN

complete the word by filling the spaces with a whole number between ONE and TEN.

F E M I _ _ _ _ _

76. NUMBER-RING

Start from the arrow and move round the circle. You have to write a number in the blank section that will continue the number pattern.

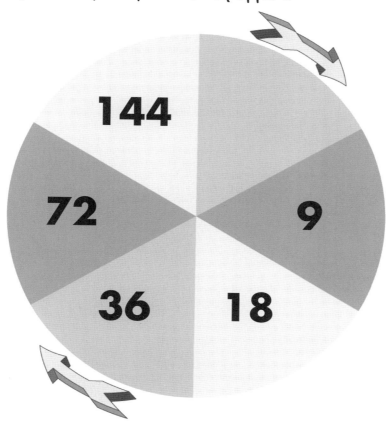

77. ADDER

Using other words with the same meaning, can you create a new word from two separate ones?

NOT ON   _ _ _

+ FROZEN WATER   _ _

= PLACE OF WORK   _ _ _ _ _

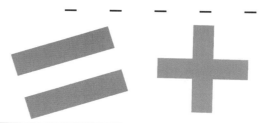

78. NUMBER FIT

Fit all the numbers back into the frame.

3 DIGITS
112 253 317 446 511 592 644 708 826 909

4 DIGITS
1177 1261 1463 1859 1902 2245 3032 3913
4420 5015 5201 6300 6377 7678 8094 9684

5 DIGITS
10803 27599 31728 73381

6 DIGITS
125630 253618 312080 462926 482572
573054 771488 890101

7 DIGITS
2968022 4373676 7222222
8117923 8835440 9052351

79. FACE FACTS

Use the letters that make up the face to make a name.

80. AFTER WORDS

Which word can go after all these words to make new words?

B E D _____

H A L F _____

S P R I N G _____

81. DOMINOES

There is something that links all the dominoes shown here. What should appear in the last domino to keep the link going?

 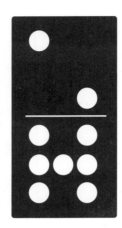 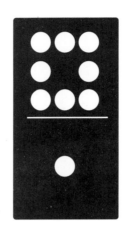 

82. MIND THE GAP

Which single three-letter word completes all of the following words?

F _ _ _ E R

B E _ _ _

A L _ _ _ E D

S _ _ _

83. SECRET SEVEN

Rearrange the letters in the words below to make another word of seven letters.

L A C E U P S

_ _ _ _ _ _ _

CLUE

Think SPACESHIP

84. TRI-PATH

Which path contains most triangles?

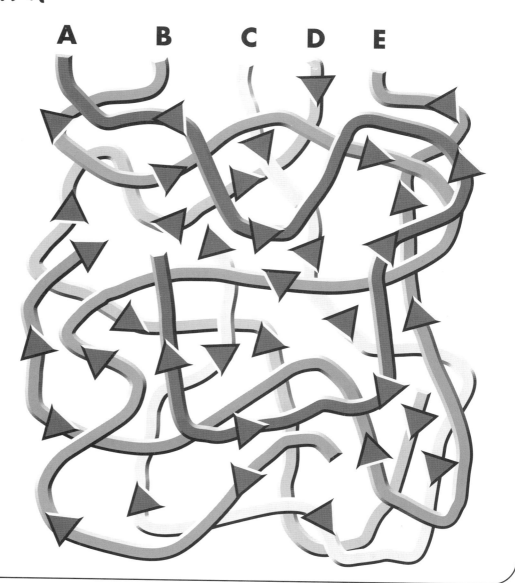

85. SIDEWAYS

What is more, the number of sides in three rectangles, or the number of sides in two pentagons?

86. LASSO

There are seven warriors on the screen. You need to make sure they can't get to each other and you have three circular force shields like the one shown. How can you position them so that every warrior is trapped?

87. ORANGE PEEL
Solve the clues. Each answer contains the same letters, plus or minus one letter.

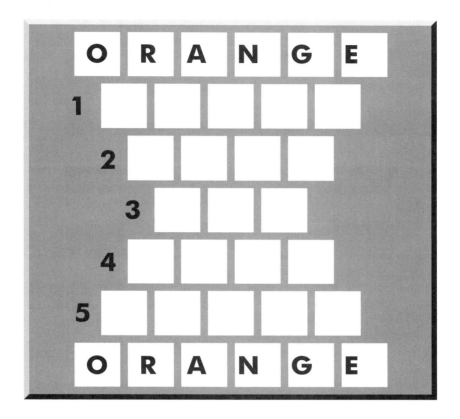

| O | R | A | N | G | E |

1. RANGE
2. RANG
3. RAG
4. GEAR
5. ANGER

| O | R | A | N | G | E |

1. Rifle shooting gallery
2. A bell sounded
3. Piece of cloth
4. Camping equipment
5. Bad temper

88. LINKS
Which word will go after the first word and before the second word?

NAVY ___   ___ JEANS

89. SPLITZER

This row of ten letters can be split into two five-letter words which are the names of two things used to make buildings. Words read from left to right and the letters are in the correct order. What are they?

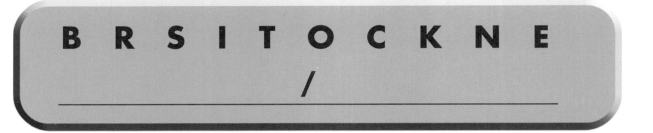

B R S I T O C K N E

/
_____

90. MUSIC BOX

Use each letter in the box to name a musical instrument.

O N P
S H X
E A O

91. ADDER

Using other words with the same meaning, can you create
a new word from two separate ones?

**OPPOSITE
OF AGAINST**

_ _ _

+ OBTAIN

_ _ _

= FAIL TO REMEMBER

_ _ _ _ _ _

92. WHAT'S NEXT?

What is the next letter to go in the space?

J

F

M

A

M

93. MIND THE GAP

Which single three-letter word completes all of the following words?

_ _ _ N E R

O R _ _ _ A R Y

_ _ _ O S A U R

94. HANDY

At the end of a show, eight children form a line at the front of the stage. As they bow to the audience they hold hands. How many hands are touching?

95. SECRET SEVEN

Rearrange the letters in the word below to make another word of seven letters.

HARICOT

_ _ _ _ _ _ _

CLUE

Think
HORSE DRAWN

96. BLOCKBACK

Fit the nine blocks back into the grid to form a completed crossword in which words interlock going either across or down.

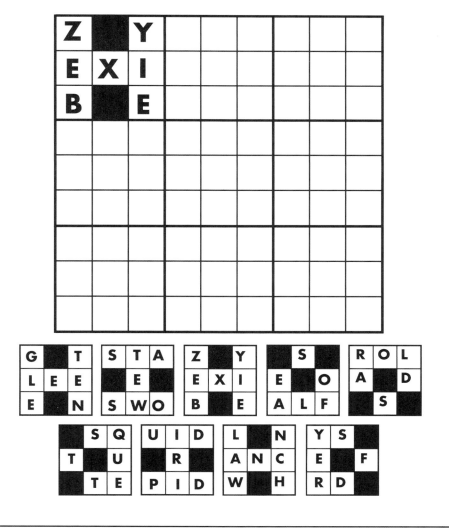

97. BACK WORDS

Solve the clues: the second answer is the first answer written backwards.

NOT COOKED * SERIES OF BATTLES

___ ___ ___ ___

*

___ ___ ___ ___

98. ROULETTE

Arrange the numbers on the roulette wheel to fill the centre circle and outer sections. Each diagonal of three numbers, always including the centre number, must add up to exactly 20. No consecutive numbers can be in touching sections of the outer wheel.

3 4 5 6 7 8 9

99. AFTER WORDS

Which word can go after all these words to make new words?

B A C K _____

C O L L A R _____

W I S H _____

100. CENTURY

Victoria is 100 years old. She's been made a special cake with 100 candles on it. Each candle will burn for exactly 3 minutes. It takes two seconds to light each candle. If there's just one person lighting the candles, will any candles have gone out by the time the hundredth is lit?

101. BACK WORDS

Solve the clues: the second answer is the first answer written backwards.

SWEET POTATO * FIFTH MONTH

_ _ _ _ _ _ * _ _ _ _

102. ABC

There is only one line that does not contain each of the letters A, B and C.
Which one is it?

1   2   3   4   5

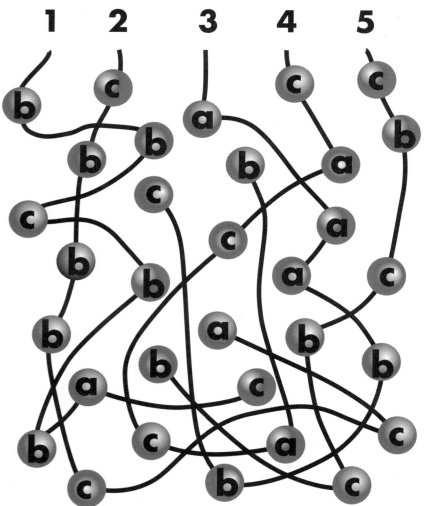

103. SECRET SEVEN

Rearrange the letters in the words below to make another word of seven letters.

CLOSE UP

_ _ _ _ _ _ _

CLUE

Think PAIRS

104. HAPPY FAMILIES

Mr and Mrs Smith have five daughters.

Each of the daughters has one brother.

All the family live in the same house.

How many people live in the Smith house?

105. MIND THE GAP

Which single three-letter word completes all of the following words?

_ _ _ _ W A R D

B E _ _ _ E

_ _ _ _ G E D

I N _ _ _ M A T I O N

106. FACE FACTS

Use the letters that make up the face to make a name.

107. AFTER WORDS
Which word can go after all these words to make new words?

B I R T H _____

S U N _____

W E E K _____

108. ADDER
Using other words with the same meaning, can you create a new word from two separate ones?

YOUNG GOAT
+ SHORT SLEEP
_____

= HOLD TO RANSOM

_ _ _
_ _ _
_ _ _ _ _

109. LINKS
Which word will go after the first word and before the second word?

W A T E R _ _ _ J U M P

110. A SLICE OF LIME

A word square reads the same whether you read it across or down. Use all these EIGHT words to make TWO word squares, with each block containing the word LIME.

AMEN
DENT
ENDS
GLAD
IRON
LIME
LIME
MOOD

111. NUMBER-RING

Move around the circle. You have to write a number in the blank section that will continue the number pattern.

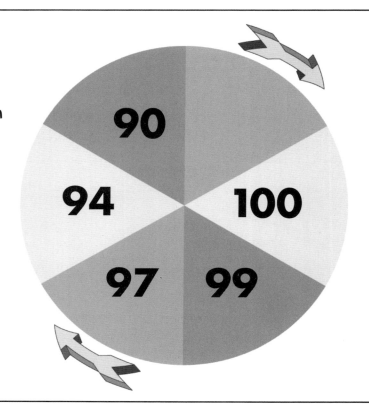

90

94   100

97   99

112. PICK A WORD

WAX   MOTTO   TOMATO

All these words have something in common. One word from the list below shares that something. Which word is it?

CHEESE   HARM
TOOTH   VERTICAL

113. CUBA

A cube is a solid shape with six sides. All these patterns contain six joined sides. No matter how hard you try, it would be impossible to construct a solid cube from most of the patterns. There's one shape that could be used to form a cube. Which one is it?

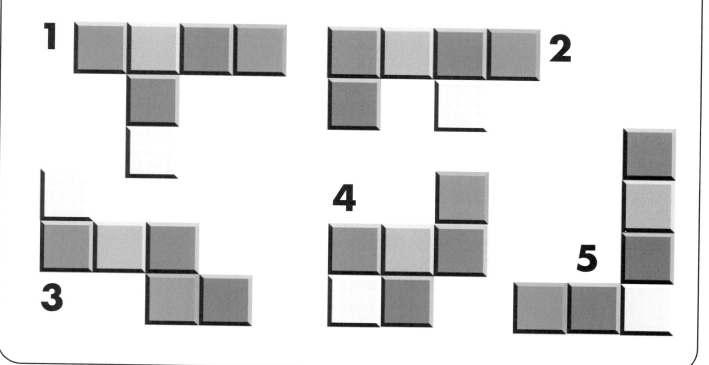

114. ALPHA-SEARCH

The aim of this puzzle is to search for the things that aren't there! Here's a jumble of letters of the alphabet. Each letter appears once, but five do not appear at all. Work out the missing letters, then arrange them to spell out the name of an animal from the wild. You need to discover 5 letters.

Animal Name

115. LOTTSA LEGS

Five cowboys are looking after a herd of cattle. If there are 150 legs altogether, how many cattle are there?

116. SPLITZER

This row of ten letters can be split into two five-letter words which are the names of two types of building. Words read from left to right and the letters are in the correct order. What are they?

H O R A N T E C H L

/ _____

117. ALL CHANGE

Solve the clues and turn the top word into the bottom one. Change just one letter with each new word.

① Person forced to work for someone else

② Remove hair or stubble from a man's chin

③ Push

④ Land by the sea

⑤ Boring and unpleasant task

⑥ Group of notes played together

S L A V E

_____

_____

_____

_____

_____

C H O R D

118. MATCHING WORD

Which word can go before all these words?

① _____ GREEN

② _____ JUICE

③ _____ SCALE

④ _____ STONE

⑤ _____ TREE

119. BACK WORDS

Solve the clues: the second answer is the first answer written backwards.

SKETCH * HOSPITAL
*
___ ___ ___ ___ ___   ___ ___ ___ ___ ___

120. PYRAMID

Fit all the words back into the pyramid grid. Each word is written in a mini-pyramid shape. The first letter of each word goes in a numbered space. The second letter goes in the space directly above, the third letter goes to the right and the fourth letter goes to the left. The word KNEE is in place to give you the idea.

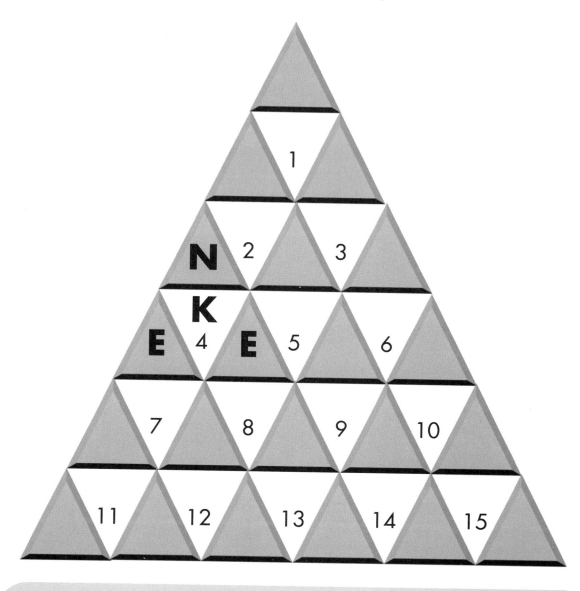

BRAG   HERE   INKY   KEEN   KNEE   NICE

OGRE   PAIR   SARI   SCAR   SIGN   STYE

TREE   WEEK   WENT

121. WHAT'S NEXT?

what is the next letter to go in the space?

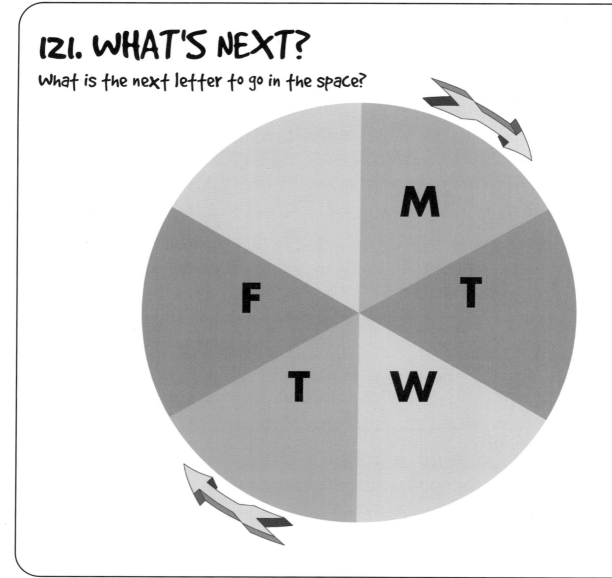

122. SECRET SEVEN

Rearrange the letters in the word below to make another word of seven letters.

C R U E L T Y

_ _ _ _ _ _ _

CLUE

Think
KNIVES AND FORKS

123. RHYMER

My first is in cheat
And also in harm.

My second's in wear
But isn't in warm.

My third is in mat
But isn't in meet.

My fourth is in three
But isn't in heat.

My fifth is in true,
But isn't in love.

There's a clue for you there
In the words up above.

124. ON LINE

Add one line to complete each letter and spell out a high tech item.

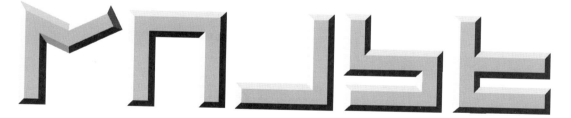

125. AFTER WORDS

Which word can go after all these words to make new words?

SEA _____ / HILL _____

OUT _____

126. BLANKS

Work out the pattern of numbers then fill in the blanks.

1 **2**
6

2 **4**
12

4 **8**
24

8

127. ADDER

Using other words with the same meaning, can you create a new word from two separate ones?

EQUIPMENT

+ NUMBER

_____

= YOUNG CAT

_ _ _

_ _ _

_ _ _ _ _ _

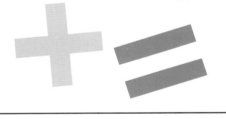

128. MIND THE GAP

Which single three-letter word completes all of the following words?

_ _ _ T E R

O R _ _ _

H A _ _ _ A T

_ _ _ E

129. MIRROR IMAGE

Here's a message as it would appear if ordinary writing was viewed in a mirror. However, on reflection, there's one letter that is not shown as an accurate mirror image. Which one is it?

WHICH LETTER
IS NOT SHOWN
CORRECTLY
HERE?

130. ON SONG

Use the words below to make two word squares. Each square must contain the word SONG.

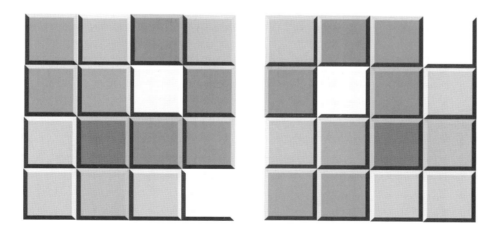

GLEE   HISS   INTO   NAME
OVAL   SONG   SONG   STUN

131. FACE FACTS

Use the letters that make up the face to make a name.

132. TOP TEN

Complete the word by filling the spaces with a whole number between ONE and TEN.

4 | A N Y _ _ _ _ | 10 8 9 3

133. MIDDLE MOVES

Each clue has two answers. The two answer words are spelt the same except that the middle letters are different.

1 Baby's bed * Slice with a knife (3 letters)

ANSWERS _____

2 With frozen water on the surface * Climbing or creeping plant (3 letters)

ANSWERS _____

3 Strike with a bat * Really warm (3 letters)

ANSWERS _____

4 An enclosed area in a building for a horse * Without moving (5 letters)

ANSWERS _____

5 Section of a book * Noisy talk (7 letters)

ANSWERS _____

134. LINKS

Which word will go after the first word and before the second word?

E G G _ _ _ _ _ _ F I S H

135. TRUE OR FALSE?

The Angel family have three boys named Andy, Bob and Carl. Their neighbours, the De Villes, also have three boys called Andy, Bob and Carl.

The Angel family always tell the truth.

The De Villes always lie.

Three boys are playing together.

Two are De Villes, the other is an Angel.

There is an Andy, a Bob and a Carl, but from which family?

Boy 1 said that his name was not Bob.

Boy 2 said that his name was not Andy.

Boy 3 said that his name was Andy.

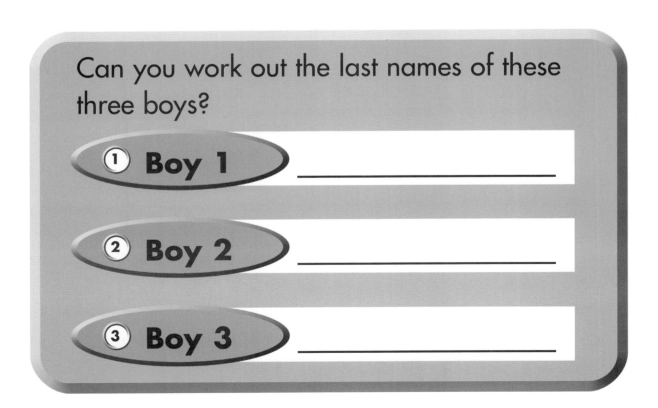

Can you work out the last names of these three boys?

① **Boy 1** _____

② **Boy 2** _____

③ **Boy 3** _____

136. SPLITZER

This row of ten letters can be split into two five-letter words which are the names of two parts of a house. Words read from left to right and the letters are in the correct order. What are they?

A F T L T I O C O R

_____ / _____

137. NUMBER-RING

Move around the circle. You have to write a number in the blank section that will continue the number pattern.

138. BACK WORDS

Solve the clues: the second answer is the first answer written backwards.

A N T E L O P E S * G R A S S

_ _ _ _ _ _ _ _ * _ _ _ _ _

139. AFTER WORDS

Which word can go after all these words to make new words?

B R E A K _____

C O U N T _____

T O U C H _____

140. SECRET SEVEN

Rearrange the letters in the word below to make another word of seven letters.

C R U I S E R
_ _ _ _ _ _ _

CLUE

Think SPICY FOOD

141. 3-4-5

fit all the listed words back into the frame.

3 Letters ARM AXE END HAS ICE
MEN TEA TIP

4 Letters ACHE ARMY DEEP DIET
EAST IDEA MELT MIND

5 Letters ALIVE ANNUL CIVIC DUVET
DWELL ELDER ENVOY EXCEL
GLOOM GRAND IDIOT INCUR
INDEX OUNCE RHYME TALLY
TOTAL VICAR

142. ADDER

Using other words with the same meaning, can you create a new word from two separate ones?

NOISE OF A COW
+ DANGER COLOUR
_____
= SECURED LIKE A BOAT

+ _ _ _

_ _ _

= _ _ _ _ _ _

143. MIND THE GAP

Which single three-letter word completes all of the following words?

T _ _ _ P

F _ _ _ E D

C _ _ _ P

S C _ _ _ B L E

144. OH BOY!

Rearrange the letters in the words below to spell out boy's names.

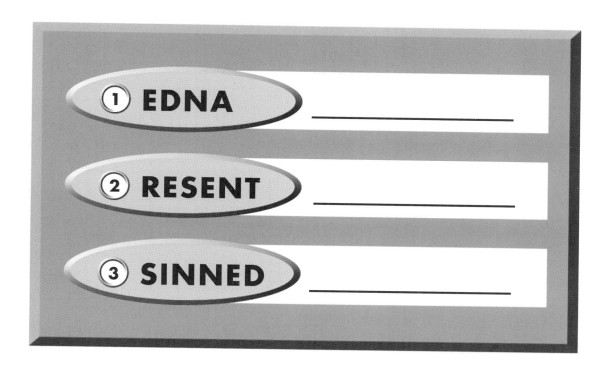

① EDNA _____

② RESENT _____

③ SINNED _____

LEVEL TWO ANSWERS

1. MOSAIC

2. AFTER-WORDS

Ship.

3. BEEP BEEP!

16. It appears six times in the units display, and ten times in the tens display.

4. OFF LINE

2, 5 and 18.

5. ON GUARD

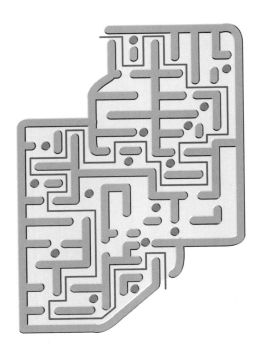

6. SECRET SEVEN

Sausage.

7. BRUSH STROKES

19.

8. MIND THE GAP

All.

9. QUARTERBACK

```
                    S O U P
                    O G R E
                    U R G E
          S L A P E E K I N D
          L O V E     I D E A
          A V O W     N E A R
          P E W S H E D A R K
                    H I V E
                    E V I L
                    D E L L
```

10. SPLITZER

Heart/Liver.

11. TRIANGLE TEST

25.

12. HONEYCOMB

1. Pirate 2. Guards 3. Rugged 4. Murder 5. Summer 6. Rivets.
The inner circle spells TAURUS.

13. BACK WORDS

Pay * Yap.

14. MORE OR LESS

The number of hours in three days (72) is more than five and a half dozen eggs, 66.

15. ADDER

Ear + Wig = Earwig.

16. CREATURE CODE

1. Rat 2. Parrot 3. Panda

17. LINKS

Port.

18. SECRET SEVEN

Batsman.

19. PICTURE GALLERY

Portrait number 11.

20. GIVE ME FIVE

1. First
2. Shell
3. Yacht
4. Storm
5. Torch
6. Pedal
7. Field
8. Three.
The word made is RECORDER.

21. CARD TRICK

The word pans read backwards reads snap.

22. LOTS OF SPOTS

S	P	O	T
P	A	V	E
O	V	A	L
T	E	L	L

O	D	D	S
D	R	O	P
D	O	D	O
S	P	O	T

I	S	L	E
S	P	O	T
L	O	A	N
E	T	N	A

23. TOP TEN

Ten. This completes the word extend.

24. WHAT'S NEXT

P. Letters are in alphabetical order, with two missed out at each move.

25. ANIMAL FILL

Ant completes the word panther.

26. TREE SURGERY

1. Bark
2. Roots
3. Branch
4. Leaf
5. Trunk.

27. SPLITZER

Eagle/Goose.

28. BLOCKS

P	U	T		T	H	E	S	E
B	L	O	C	K	S		I	N
T	H	E		F	R	A	M	E
S	O		T	H	A	T		A
S	E	N	T	E	N	C	E	
I	S		F	O	R	M	E	D

29. ON LINE

Computer.

30. NICE MICE

1. Mice
2. Rice
3. Race
4. Face
5. Fare
6. Fire
7. File
8. Mile.

31. LINKS

Whale.

32. ON TARGET

17 + 24 + 39 = 80.

33. AFTER WORDS

Line.

34. NUMBER-RING

28. 5 is added each time.

35. SECRET SEVEN

Bedroom.

36. PAIRS

2 and 5.

37. MIND THE GAP

Bat.

38. MORE OR LESS

The number of sides in four octagons, 32,
is more than the sides in nine triangles, 27.

39. BACK WORDS

Pit * Tip.

40. SNAKES ALIVE!

1. Adder

2. Cobra

3. Boa.

41. SPIDER'S WEB

42. NATIONWIDE

1. Peru
2. Spain
3. Nepal
4. Yemen.

43. ADDER

Leg + End = Legend.

44. FACE FACTS

Polly.

45. SECRET SEVEN

Lobster.

46. OWL SIGNS

1. owl
2. wolf
3. foal
4. fox.

47. MIND THE GAP

Pal.

48. LINKS

Bow.

49. BACK WORDS

Pot * Top.

50. ON THE MAP
Map c.

51. SQUASHED SANDWICHES!
1. Cheese
2. Tuna
3. Chicken
4. Salad
5. Prawn.

52. SECRET SEVEN
Carpets.

53. 3D

54. PATTERN PLAY
No 3. The other patterns have the same features in the same order.

55. ADDER
Fat + Her = Father.

56. STARGAZER

1. Flan
2. Foam
3. Flow
4. Wolf
5. Farm
6. Warn.

57. COMPUTER CODE

Mouse.

58. MIND THE GAP

Sit.

59. LEMON-AID

13 times.

60. AFTER WORDS

Word.

61. ROUNDABOUT

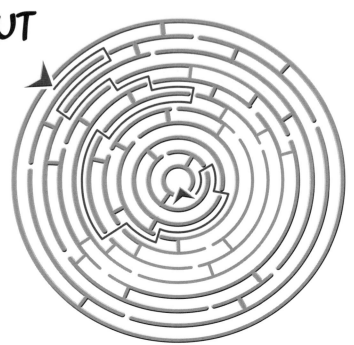

62. LINKS

Chest.

63. CAPITAL, CAPITAL

1. Madrid
2. Paris
3. Athens
4. Rome
5. Cairo
6. Berlin.

64. FRUITY

Peach. Take the letters PE (half of PEAR), A (middle of GRAPE) and CH (one third of CHERRY).

65. WHAT AM I?

Table.

66. MORE OR LESS

The number of days in May doubled is 62, which is more than the 52 fortnights that are in two years.

67. ALPHA-NUMBERS

1. Eleven
2. Eight
3. Twelve
4. Thirty
5. Fourteen.

68. SPLITZER

Canoe/Yacht.

69. FAST TRACK

A Tom ran 200 m and finished third.

B Rachel ran 400 m and finished last.

C Sarah ran 100 m and finished first.

D Robin ran 800 m and finished second.

70. BACKWORDS

Rat * Tar.

71. IN THE MIDDLE

1. L
2. E
3. M
4. O
5. N. LEMON

72. YOUR DEAL

5, 6, 7 and 8.

73. COMPU-COMMAND

Open.

74. MOONS

They are both the same size.

75. TOP TEN

Nine. This completes the word feminine.

76. NUMBER-RING

288. Each number is doubled.

77. ADDER

Off + Ice = office.

78. NUMBER FIT

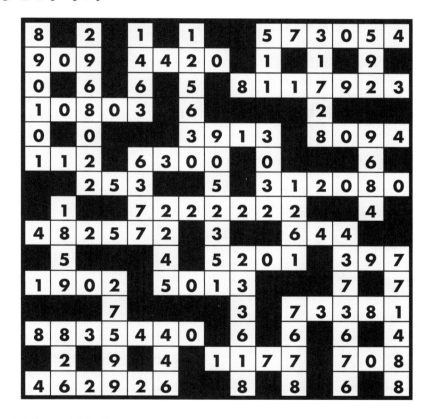

79. FACE FACTS

Timothy.

80. AFTER WORDS

Time.

81. DOMINOES

Five dots. All the dominoes have nine dots.

82. MIND THE GAP

Low.

83. SECRET SEVEN

capsule.

84. TRI-PATH

Path C. It contains eight triangles.

85. SIDEWAYS

The number of sides in three rectangles, 12, is more than the 10 sides in two pentagons.

86. LASSO

87. ORANGE PEEL

1. Range
2. Rang
3. Rag
4. Gear
5. Anger.

88. LINKS

Blue.

89. SPLITZER

Brick/Stone.

90. MUSIC BOX

Saxophone.

91. ADDER

For + Get = Forget.

92. WHAT'S NEXT?

J for June. They are the first letters of months of the year.

93. MIND THE GAP

Din.

94. HANDY

14.

95. SECRET SEVEN

Chariot.

96. BLOCKBACK

97. BACK WORDS

Raw * war.

98. ROULETTE

99. AFTER WORDS

Bone.

100. CENTURY

Yes. It will take 200 seconds to light them all.
Each candle burns for three minutes — that's 180 seconds.

101. BACK WORDS

Yam * May.

102. ABC

Line s.

103. SECRET SEVEN

Couples.

104. HAPPY FAMILIES

Eight. Two parents, five daughters and one son.

105. MIND THE GAP

For.

106. FACE FACTS

Fiona.

107. AFTER WORDS

Day.

108. ADDER

Kid + Nap = Kidnap.

109. LINKS

Ski.

110. A SLICE of LIME

Lime, Iron, Mood, Ends.
Glad, Lime, Amen, Dent.

111. NUMBER-RING

85. 1 is taken away, then 2, then 3, then 4, then 5.

112. PICK A WORD

TooTH. The shape of the letters is the link.
Each letter in each word is symmetrical. The left half is a mirror image of the right half.

113. CUBA

No 3.

114. ALPHA-SEARCH

Zebra.

115. LoTTSA LEGS

35.

116. SPLITZER

Hotel/Ranch.

117. ALL CHANGE

1. Slave
2. Shave
3. Shove
4. Shore
5. Chore
6. Chord.

118. MATCHING WORD

Lime.

119. BACK WORDS

Draw * ward.

120. PYRAMID

121. WHAT'S NEXT?

S. They are the first letters of days of the week.

122. SECRET SEVEN

cutlery.

123. RHYMER

Heart.

124. ON LINE

Mouse.

125. AFTER WORDS

Side.

126. BLANKS

48 goes inside the triangle. 16 goes outside. All the numbers are doubled with each triangle.

127. ADDER

Kit + Ten = Kitten.

128. MIND THE GAP

Bit.

129. MIRROR IMAGE

The L from CORRECTLY.

130. ON SONG

S	O	N	G
O	V	A	L
N	A	M	E
G	L	E	E

H	I	S	S
I	N	T	O
S	T	U	N
S	O	N	G

131. FACE FACTS

Charlie.

132. TOP TEN

one. This completes the word anyone.

133. MIDDLE MOVES

1. Cot Cut
2. Icy Ivy
3. Hit Hot
4. Stall Still
5. Chapter Chatter.

134. LINKS

Shell.

135. TRUE OR FALSE?

Boy 1 is Carl Angel. He tells the truth.

Boy 2 is Andy De Villes, who lies.

Boy 3 is Bob De Villes, who lies.

136. SPLITZER

Attic/floor.

137. NUMBER-RING

243. Numbers are multiplied by 3.

138. BACK WORDS

Deer * Reed.

139. AFTER WORDS

Down.

140. SECRET SEVEN

Curries.

141. 3-4-5

142. ADDER

Moo + Red = Moored.

143. MIND THE GAP

Ram.

144. OH BOY!

1. Dean 2. Ernest 3. Dennis.